Journey
to the Heart

Journey
to the Heart

Nora Caron

HOMEBOUND
PUBLICATIONS
Independent Publisher of Contemplative Titles

PUBLISHED BY HOMEBOUND PUBLICATIONS

For information or permissions write: Homebound Publications,
PO Box 1442, Pawcatuck, Connecticut 06379 United States of America

THIRD EDITION
ISBN: 978-1-938846-09-0 (pbk)

First Published in 2008 and 2009 by Fisher King Press

WWW.HOMEBOUNDPUBLICATIONS.COM
VISIT THE AUTHOR AT: WWW. NORACARON.COM

BOOK DESIGN
Front Cover Image: © Brykaylo Yuriy [shutterstock.com]
Cover and Interior Design: Leslie M. Browning

Library of Congress Cataloging-in-Publication Data

Caron, Nora, 1981-
Journey to the heart / Nora Caron. — Third edition
    pages cm
ISBN 978-1-938846-09-0 (pbk.)
1. Women computer programmers—Fiction. 2. Canadians—Mexico—Fiction. 3. Identity (Psychology)—Fiction. I. Title.
PR9199.4.C3725J98 2013
813'.6—dc23

                                        2013001592

10 9 8 7 6 5 4 3

Part One
Openings

Chapter 1

The soft morning light streamed into the bright pink hotel room, giving Lucina some comfort. At least the weather seemed to be in a better mood than her. She threw her hairbrush onto the single narrow bed, grabbed her heavy brown leather purse, and slammed the hotel door shut.

"Breakfast time!" she pronounced to the emptiness around her.

Lucina had only been in Oaxaca City for a day and had not had the opportunity to explore much of the marketplace. She looked forward to hitting the little art stands she had seen the night before while she was going through the city by bus. But first, breakfast had to be taken care of. The only restaurant near the hotel was a little Italian coffee shop and that suited Lucina just fine. She sauntered in, ignored the Spanish sign asking for clients to wait for seating, and selected an isolated round table near the large sunny window overlooking Santa Domingo church. The coffee shop was nearly empty, except for a heavy older Mexican man, sitting with his feet up on a chair in the corner, puffing away at his thick cigar.

A short grinning middle-aged Spanish woman appeared and asked politely in English what Lucina wished to order. The waitress looked as though she had taken too much coffee that morning; her thin hands fluttered to her head-band, tried to straighten it out nervously, and a nervous twitch appeared near her upper lip. It was disconcerting to look at her, so Lucina concentrated on the menu.

"I would like two eggs, two toasts, and strong, black coffee," Lucina said, avoiding looking at the waitress.

"*No problema, no problema, no problema,*" the waitress said, bowing as she left, still trying to straighten out her silly headband.

Lucina sighed, put her hands to her forehead, and closed her eyes. *Alone on vacation, how amusing,* she thought. *Alone after a burn-out, with nobody but me, myself and I. Doctor Field should have prescribed some travelling assistant while he was at it.*

"Lucina, vacations need to be taken when we are empty," he had said during the last session. "Do you know what you have done to your body with all your work? You have burnt it, that's what you've done, and the only way to repair it, is go to a sunshine country. I recommend Mexico; the people there are friendly and the energy is good."

"Doctor Field, I don't need a vacation, I need to get this bastard back!" Lucina had answered angrily. His look had silenced her. He had walked over to the tape player, lifted a finger to indicate that it was quiet time, and pressed play. A soft melody had begun to play in the speakers.

"Lie down, Lucina, and close your eyes. Anger is no good, we talked about this *last* week. Now breathe, that's it, breathe."

Oh, good old Doctor Field, Lucina thought sadly. *Where is he when I need someone to talk to?*

Breakfast arrived. Lucina ate forcefully, chewing slowly and swallowing with difficulty. *Food lost its attraction a long time ago,* she concluded. *What is the point of eating if you no longer have the desire to live?*

A good-looking Asian couple passed by the large window at that moment, laughing and holding hands. Lucina groaned inwardly and stared at her black coffee. *Blackness is my friend,* she mused. *There it is, not moving, not talking, just being. I wish I were blackness itself. Then I could maybe pass off as being some-*

thing other than empty and dead inside.

After paying for the tasteless food, Lucina strolled out to the market square and began to look around with more interest. Although it was still quite early in the morning, 7 a.m., the life in Oaxaca City had begun a long time ago. Children played in the water fountains, older people sat under the shade of giant trees, barely talking to each other. Hand-made Mayan clothing was spread out on Mexican blankets on the ground and a few tourists scrutinized the contents on slanted plastic tables, trying to bargain with the local artisans.

Lucina began to feel less negative as she looked around the town square. Sometimes being around strangers does that to people; it takes away the feeling that one is alone in the blackness and temporarily removes fears and anxieties. *Where there is life, there is hope,* Lucina reminded herself. Doctor Field had always taught her that.

She walked randomly into a near-by jewelry store, roamed through the tiny little aisles, and squeezed her way around large, noisy Americans. Finding nothing that interested her, she wandered back outside. Suddenly, a tiny little shop next to the jewelry store caught her eye.

"*Libros de la Vida Azul,*" Lucina muttered out loud. Curious, she pushed the faded screen door and walked in. Lucina had always liked books, but had read little of the great literature that permeated bookstores. Her sense of literature was limited to the Grimm fairy tales which she had always liked better than Walt Disney movies, as well as some Gothic novels that had stimulated her sexual appetite from time to time as a teenager.

Heavy Indian incense greeted her as she walked cautiously in. Lucina noticed the little aisles crammed to the ceiling with hundreds of books and smelt the faint odor of dust in the stifled air. Lastly, she saw the woman behind the cluttered counter near the small window looking out on the market square. The woman was a large, imposing Mexican with long, black hair and big, brown, glittering eyes.

"*Buenos días, hermana,*" the Mexican said in a deep, almost masculine voice. Lucina stood still, curious as to why she had been greeted as a sister when obviously she was not Mexican but Canadian.

"*Buenos días,*" she reciprocated politely.

Lucina was, for some reason, very uncomfortable under the stranger's gaze, so she immediately headed for a corner where the woman couldn't watch her. When she realized that she was in the yoga and spirituality section, she steered abruptly back to the computer and science sections and picked up a random book. *How rude to stare at customers like that,* she thought, feeling annoyed. *In Montreal, people bother you but at least they don't stare and make you uncomfortable.*

"Are you looking for something in particular?" rang the woman's deep voice again, this time in a light English accent.

"No, just looking."

"Would you like to read some Carlos Castaneda perhaps? I have here his *Art of Dreaming,* a very good read. It helps one realize dreams are more than dreams."

Carlos who? Lucina muttered a loud "no thanks" and carefully moved towards the exit. *I need to get out of here as fast as possible,* she was thinking in a panic. As she was about to squeeze her way through the screen door, a hand landed on her shoulder, causing Lucina to nearly drop her few shopping bags.

"*Hermana,* always look both ways before crossing the road," said the book woman, looking down at her with a statue-like brown face.

Utterly at a loss for words, Lucina mumbled a faint "thanks" and took off down the bustling street. Anxiously, she turned to look over her shoulder several times to make sure that she was not being followed by the imposing woman. *Do witches still exist?* she found herself thinking. *Doctor Field could have at least mentioned the weirdos before suggesting Oaxaca City. I could have been murdered back there. Do Mexicans eat people? I wouldn't be surprised if they did. You never know these days, what with all the weird events happening all over the world.*

Sighing, Lucina took up her daily exploration and made her way back to the town square named the *Zócalo*. Opting for a bench in the shade away from the bustle, she sat down and pulled out a thick blue diary. Writing in a diary had become a daily routine since the burn-out. As a child, Lucina's godmother had given her her first diary and had told her that whenever the world was too much to handle, writing would find a way to guide her. Doctor Field had also encouraged Lucina to continue writing in a diary, explaining to her that writing was an excellent introspection exercise.

"Writing is wonderful; it allows our demons room to debate amongst themselves," he had said to her, laughing out loud.

Lucina took out a ball-point pen, settled herself comfortably, and started jotting down fleeting thoughts. The noise of the market square slowly vanished and she found herself immersed in her thoughts, miles away from the awakening city life.

Dear Diary,   December 2nd

It was a nice plane ride to Mexico City yesterday. I didn't sleep on the plane, but found a nice spot to sleep on the bus going to Oaxaca. So far, the weather has been warm and not too hot. I find myself wondering what I'm supposed to do with myself here. I

speak Spanish well enough, but I don't want to talk
to people that much. Talking is something that drains
me these days, plus I feel as though no one understands me anyhow. What is the point of talking when
only air comes out?

I guess having a burn-out might have something
to do with the fact that I don't want to speak. I feel
tired and grumpy most of the time. Doctor Field kept
telling me before my departure, "Flow and let go, flow
and let go," but I don't think I know how to let go.
There are so many things I need to let go of; let go of
Lincoln, let go of my old job, let go of the pain and
tears of the last months.

Where do I begin?

"Estás escribiendo un libro, señora?" a young voice asked
Lucina, snapping her out of her silent world. She looked up at
a young Mexican boy and smiled.

"No, I'm not writing a book, only a journal," she replied
in Spanish.

"You look like a writer, with your nice pants and shoes," he
commented, grinning.

"Really? Why, thank you." Lucina stared at the reclining
figure of the boy. To be young, innocent, and happy, *that* was
what she really wanted. She didn't want to be twenty five with
a serious case of depression and lack of financial stability, not
to mention bad luck with all men who happened to cross her
path.

"Bloody life," Lucina muttered to herself, slamming the
diary shut. She didn't feel like writing anymore. What was
there for her to say other than, life sucks?

*   *   *

At around 3 p.m., Lucina bought some burritos from a nearby stand, a few fruit and vegetables, and decided to head back to the tranquil hotel near the Santa Domingo church.

My introspection has not been that productive up to now, she was thinking sadly to herself. *Maybe I should give it a few more days, maybe I'm just not inspired enough.*

All of a sudden, Lucina noticed the bizarre book woman sitting on a bench nearby. The woman was reading a book and seemed absorbed in the novel. Lucina's first instinct was to duck behind an old German couple, in order to hide from the intimidating stranger. *I don't need another encounter with witches,* she mused, observing the stranger from afar. *I don't think I can handle these types of people.*

"*Ach Gott, Wilhelm, was hast du gesagt? Das Wetter ist perfekt. Du jammerst immer wie ein kleines Kind!*" the woman was saying to her husband. The man shrugged, looked angry, and stared straight ahead of him, ignoring his wife.

Lucina's endeavour to conceal herself, however, was in vain. Abruptly, the woman looked up right at her and a half smile appeared on her thick lips. *Oh God, not another trip to the Twilight Zone,* Lucina moaned inwardly. The Mexican waved Lucina over. Smiling uncertainly and feeling like she wanted to vanish off the face of the planet, Lucina nonetheless ventured over to where the stranger was sitting.

"Please, sit down," the woman said in her soft English accent, watching Lucina like a hawk. Lucina sat down nervously and placed her shopping bags on the ground next to her. Silence hit. Lucina tried to think of something to say to make the awkwardness go away.

"Please, tell me what you meant when you said, 'Look both ways before crossing the road'. Are you some sort of fortune teller?" Lucina said at last, feeling at a loss for words.

"Even if I were, you would not believe me. No, Señorita, I

am only like you, someone in search of answers. What I meant was that there are always two opposite directions in life, but all roads cross at *you*."

"Pardon me?"

"Ah, you Americans…"

"Canadians, please, Canadians."

"Canadians," she resumed, "You are all the same. You do not get it right away: Too intellectual, too caught in the head, not enough in the stomach and heart."

Lucina decided not to resume the topic seeing that they were getting off on a bad start, and she certainly didn't want to be on the bad side of a witch. Cautiously, she asked where the stranger lived. The Mexican replied that she lived ten minutes out of town, on a quiet little property, far from the noise of the city.

"Oh, that sounds nice," Lucina said trying to imagine what kind of house the stranger lived in. Probably a cave of some sort, with books piled to the ceiling, herbs in big glass jars, and a few dead animals hanging from the ceiling. "I am staying at Posada Margarita, do you know of it?"

The Mexican didn't reply. Lucina fidgeted in her seat, trying to look calm when in reality, her heart was beating furiously in her chest and her palms were sweaty. The woman looked up at Lucina then and smiled. Her big yellow teeth caught the early afternoon sun.

"Do you like camping?" she asked.

"Camping?"

"Yes, camping."

"Ah, I guess so, yes, I do," Lucina answered, wondering where the conversation was leading this time.

The woman paused, looking as though she was thinking hard about something. She chewed on her thick lip and mumbled to herself in Spanish.

"Yes, camping. I have a big land and tourists often like to camp on my land. I do not charge anything, except I ask that people help me on my land, to take care of my plants and things like this. Are you interested in camping on my land?"

Lucina began to feel the laughter rising. Laughter was Lucina's mechanism of defence. When things would get out of hand, Lucina would laugh like a silly child. One time, her best friend had fallen from a bike and split her knee open and instead of flipping out, Lucina had burst out laughing and her friend had been greatly offended. That was how Lucina dealt with unexpected, scary things in life: She would laugh like an idiot.

Camping on this weird woman's land? Lucina pondered. *I don't even have a tent. And camping entails weird insects, such as big, Mexican spiders, and also flies and other strange things that fly. Camping means cold showers, and sleeping on the hard ground, and waking up feeling stiff and old and crabby. Camping means being afraid that some crazy Mexicans might break into my tent, and kill me during my sleep.*

Lucina's facial expression must have given her away, for the woman patted her arm reassuringly.

"Don't worry, it's very comfortable, my tent," she continued, seriously.

Lucina wasn't the least reassured. Why was this stranger inviting her over? Did she want to murder her, make her into some human burrito or something?

Doctor Field's words echoed in Lucina's head at that moment.

"Lucina, the minute you feel your old feelings of paranoia creep up, stomp on them! Stomp on them, like we are doing!" and he had leaped out of his arm chair and actually slammed his foot down on the floor. But Lucina had known better: It wasn't as easy as some people thought. Anxiety was not something that just vanished into thin air, it was not something you could brush under the carpet and hope no one would notice. People noticed her anxiety.

"Doctor Field, I don't know how to shut the voices in my head," Lucina had replied, looking sadly at him. Mozart's flute concerto was playing in the background, trying to soothe her tired mind.

"You simply tell them to fuck off," he had answered, giving Lucina a big grin.

Good old Doctor Field, he had known all about the injustices. She had told him about how her boss had fired her and stolen her invention, her own original programming invention which would have made her rich. Doctor Field had been kind and sympathetic and he had known what to say to her.

At least someone knew how to talk to her.

Somehow, at that moment, despite her fear of the woman, Lucina knew that she couldn't let her old self take over and ruin things again. She didn't want to return to those patterns. She stared a few long seconds more into the Mexican's burning eyes and tried to relax. *If I am going to get over the past and the fears, I have to start somewhere, right?* she convinced herself.

Hesitantly, Lucina told the woman that she would accept her proposal but that she really wanted to pay for the stay. The stranger held up a large hand and shook her head, explaining that she never accepted money; rather, she would accept help with planting and weeding on her property. Lucina explained hesitantly that she knew nothing of plants, that she was a computer programmer in Montreal, not a weeder.

"You cannot help me with that. I hate computers. They are vile things and deserve to be burnt," grunted the woman loudly. "No, rather you will do yard work. Yes?"

"Fine, that's fine with me. Thank you very much," Lucina answered somewhat shakily, still shocked that she was accepting such a proposition from a woman who obviously was not normal to Canadian standards.

"I live at *78 Calle de los Aves.* Come early tomorrow morning and we will eat breakfast together. You can take the 45 bus, it stops right next to my street. *Hasta mañana,"* said the Mexican as she got up to leave.

Lucina moved aside and watched her walk away with her book in hand, still filled with scepticism and fear.

What the hell am I doing? I am probably losing my mind altogether, Lucina thought sadly. *Well, it doesn't matter since I have nothing to lose anymore anyhow.*

*   *   *

When Lucina returned to the peaceful Posada Margarita, it was already dark outside. She walked through the front white wooden gate and quietly made her way to the room situated in the back of the courtyard. It seemed like she was the only tourist in the little hotel, which was odd because it was nearly Christmas, the big season in Mexico. The tourists were probably all in Cancun, sipping on cocktails, receiving massages, and eating fatty foods.

After putting the food on the counter, Lucina sat down in the over-sized faded brown leather sofa chair and closed her blue eyes. The only sound was the ceiling fan, swishing respectfully above the bed.

Out of nowhere appeared Mr. Steve's face, floating in the mirror in the bathroom.

"Men are the source of all evil," Lucina muttered to the darkness. "The world would be a much better place without them. We should have sperm banks and that's it."

She took a bite from a red juicy apple and munched loudly in the semi-darkness. The apparition vanished from the mirror.

Chapter 2

Lucina stood at the crossroads of *78 Calle de los Aves* and the main road, watching the bus drive away with her bags in hand and a slightly nauseous feeling. She straightened up, taking a deep breath, trying to calm her body.

After having explained to the owner of Posada Margarita that there was nothing wrong with the hotel, that she simply wanted to try camping, Lucina had taken the early bus to meet the strange woman for breakfast. She wasn't sure what she was doing standing in front of a stranger's house, but she felt like her life was about to get more interesting.

78 Calle de los Aves was more a yellow shack than a house. The porch sagged, the windows were cracked, the roof looked like it was about to cave in, and the paint was peeling. A thick, spiky green carpet surrounded the dwelling, and here and there coconut trees offered some shade. The area looked rather peaceful, and since there didn't seem to be too many neighbors, Lucina concluded that it was indeed an attractive change and certainly more exciting than a hotel.

Maybe this was what Doctor Field had meant when he had told her at the last therapy session that life was like a river, that one had to learn how to let go of the shore and let the current do the pulling. Lucina had not understood it at first.

"But I don't even know if I'm in the water or on dry land, Doctor Field!" she had replied.

"Lucina, we are all in the water; some have it up to their knees and others have it above their heads. I think you are the latter. Just remember that if you stop fighting with the water, you will float. Humans float naturally, we seem to constantly forget this."

How I wish I could have his advice right now, she thought. *Where is the shore now, miles away or a few feet away?*

"*Hola*, señorita," called out a familiar deep voice from behind her.

Lucina spun around and came face to face with the short, over-weight brown-skinned woman. The Mexican that day wore a faded sleeveless red summer dress, a wide straw hat, and carried some dark roots in her left hand. Her stringy long black hair fluttered around her bulky body in a rather eerie manner. *A real witch*, Lucina mused. *What do I have to wear to protect myself from witches? I know vampires don't like garlic, but what do witches not like?*

"*Hola*, señora..."

"Señora Labotta."

"*Encantado*, I'm Lucina Pilano," Lucina replied, relieved at the formal introductions at last.

Labotta it was. The two women looked at each other for a few long seconds. Finally, Señora Labotta walked past Lucina unto the rickety porch, pointing to a small table and some run-down white plastic chairs to the left. The porch was a good forty feet long by twenty feet across. Above it was a decaying roof, which apparently nested a variety of bird species if one looked closely at the many different nests scattered underneath it. A few large pots decorated the four corners of the porch, and in them grew a variety of exotic, colorful flowers, none of which Lucina recognized. Flowers had never been an interest to her; she couldn't even take care of a cactus. The last cactus had dried up years ago and she had left it on the window sill as a reminder never to buy another plant in her life again.

"Sit, and we will have *huevos a la mexicana*," Señora Labotta said loudly before slamming the screen door shut. Lucina looked down at the square-shaped wooden table and did a double take. There, staring back at her, was a pair of huge golden eyes.

"Like my eyes?" said Señora Labotta, walking out a few seconds later with a tray of delicious smelling food. "They are the eyes of the conscience."

Lucina nodded and looked again at the golden eyes, dropping her bags at the same time. She waited for Señora Labotta to sit before sitting herself down at the tiny table. The two women began to eat breakfast, Lucina observing how the woman ate quietly and cautiously. Although the eggs tasted delicious, she was careful not to eat too quickly in order to be polite.

A few minutes later, the stranger asked Lucina what she thought of the eyes on the table. Lucina, confused, didn't know what to reply at first, so Señora Labotta explained that she wanted to know what she thought the eyes reminded her guest of. Lucina, still bewildered, fumbled for an answer, and at last blurted out that the eyes looked angry.

"Angry eyes? Are you angry, Lucina?" Señora Labotta asked quietly.

Lucina gulped down her orange juice and didn't look up. *What is that for a question? Do I have to answer?* she pondered. *It's really none of her business.* Doctor Field's words returned to her, louder this time, "Flow and let go, flow and let go". She at last decided there was no harm in answering the question affirmatively. Señora Labotta prodded her further: Why was she angry? Lucina looked up at the stranger, her anxiety bubbling up inside her. Whenever her anxiety started, Lucina felt as though her stomach was being compressed, and she hated the feeling.

Señora Labotta looked tranquil, nonchalant, which gave Lucina the confidence to explain her reasons for being angry. In a paragraph, Lucina summed up how her boss had fired her from her computer programming job, how fear had driven her last love away, and how now she was mentally and physically exhausted. Señora Labotta nodded the whole time, looking deep in thought.

"Lucina, which cat over there is the male and which cat is the female?" Señora Labotta questioned. Lucina looked up, turned around, and observed the two cats sleeping on a love-seat at the other end of the porch. She shook her head, more confused than ever.

"I don't know," she replied.

"There you go," sighed the Mexican, pulling her hair back from her slightly wrinkled face. "Sex is a secondary issue. What matters is that there are two cats and they are next to each other. You have hate against men, but it's not men you hate: It's stupid, ignorant souls."

Lucina swallowed more orange juice. *Keep busy and look cool,* she reassured herself. *This woman is just a freak, I shouldn't tell her too much about my life.*

"In your country," continued Señora Labotta, "people only see sex. They do not see the soul, only the sex. You hit some bad human shells in the past few years, and it happened to be male shells. Get over it. Life is like that."

Lucina gaped at the stranger in front of her for some time, and then reminded herself how impolite it was to be staring. *She certainly has a way with words,* Lucina mused, *and she certainly lacks politeness, yet there is something quite honest about her.* Nervously, Lucina replied that maybe she was right, but that most humans who were rotten were men. Men made war, raped women, beat their wives, and couldn't be gentle if their lives depended on it.

Sighing, Señora Labotta shook her head and patiently explained to her guest that since men shells were the ones in power in this time and age, and had been for quite a while, it was normal that they did as they pleased. Women shells would reign again, she promised Lucina, and when the time would come, men shells would become the second sex again, as they had been at the beginning of time.

Incredulous that they finally agreed on something, Lucina asked her why she believed women would rule again. The Mexican woman was quiet and then slowly answered that women shells had suffered enough, and that now the tables would turn. The two women were silent for several minutes. The only sound was the sound of distant birds chirping in the jungle behind the yellow house. Lucina looked up at the mysterious woman. *Whatever has made me come to this place and be with a person like this?* she thought. *Is it destiny? Do I even believe in destiny?*

"What is important is that you go beyond the shells of humans," the Mexican emphasized, putting her fork down. "Do not blame men. Their souls contain both sexes. You should say that there are many rotten souls in the bodies of men and that would be more justified. There is no point in hating a shell. It is useless, believe me, a complete waste of time."

That's true, Lucina thought to herself. *Perhaps I should start looking beyond shells, into the soul of people. Maybe Mr. Steve and all my previous boyfriends were just bad souls. I must have some sort of bad karma or something. What is karma anyways?* Lucina pondered, realizing she didn't even know what she was thinking about.

*   *   *

After breakfast, Señora Labotta helped Lucina carry her things to a large, somewhat beat-up white four-person tent near a grove of coconut trees. The spot looked cozy and private, just what Lucina had hoped for. Señora Labotta excused herself, saying that she had things to do, but told her guest that she could unpack and make herself at home.

Lucina threw her various possessions into her new sleeping quarters, but stopped dead in her tracks when she spotted another little tent through the low bushes some thirty feet away from her tent. Intrigued, she put her bags down and ventured towards the other mysterious tent, all the while looking attentively around her. *One can never be too careful,* she was thinking. *It could always be a gringo, or some other crazy Mexican person waiting to pump me full of lead, just like in the movies.*

"*Hola!*" said a male voice from behind Lucina.

She whirled around to face the intruder, putting her fists up to her face automatically. When she saw who it was, she lowered her fists and started to feel embarrassed. Doctor Field had told her not to over-react, why couldn't she follow simple advice? She had to stop being paranoid. She shook her head a little, dropping her hands into her jean pockets. *It seems that kung fu lessons still come in handy,* she mused.

"Whoa, I am not a burglar, you can relax!" the man replied, laughing.

"*Hola,*" Lucina answered, giving him a quick, annoyed glance.

The man looked no more than thirty, had a warm smile, and brown coffee skin. His emerald, green eyes stared back at Lucina innocently, as if asking her why she was not more welcoming. As he walked closer to her, she couldn't help but notice the silkiness of his raven-colored curly hair, which stopped just above his broad shoulders.

"Is *that* your tent?" Lucina asked him, pointing to the green one-person igloo tent some thirty feet away.

"Yes, it is," said the man in a good English accent, holding out his hand. "I'm here visiting my mother. I'm Teleo."

Lucina was so shocked that she stared at him and didn't respond for a few seconds. A man was staying here, close to her, and that woman had never warned her. This was terrible! At that moment, she wanted to pack her things immediately and return to her peaceful hotel room.

"Nice to meet you, my name is Lucina," she said rapidly, shaking his hand quickly and firmly. *That is the last thing I need,* Lucina thought in a panic. *Another horny man prancing around near my terrain, trying to seduce me with roses and ballads and God knows what other tactics.*

Lucina had had enough of romance in her days, enough to fill a novel.

Teleo wished her a good day, explaining that he had errands to run for his mother. Lucina was not surprised that he had errands to run for that woman.

"Teleo. What an odd name. Everything is odd around here," she muttered to herself as she made her way back to the larger tent. "I hope he won't bother me playing guitar or something. Those Mexicans are known for partying all night, and being a man, he might want to make noise all night."

*   *   *

Sometime later, Lucina spotted Señora Labotta in the backyard and hesitantly offered to help with some yard work. The Mexican smiled, handed over a pair of cutters and a green garbage bag, and indicated what needed to be weeded. Since Lucina looked lost as to which plants were weeds and which were flowers, the woman gave her a short five minute botany course.

"Some plants look like flowers, like this one," Señora Labotta said, yanking out a long, purple flowery plant. "But in reality they are weeds and don't belong here. Sometimes it is hard to tell weeds from flowers, but once you recognize the weeds, you cannot be fooled any longer."

Rather reluctantly, Lucina began pulling weeds out from the flower beds. Nodding in satisfaction, Señora Labotta left her to her task and returned to the kitchen to prepare the supper. Lucina worked hard for two hours, pulling out random plants, hoping they were weeds. Feeling good about the accomplishment, she went to see the Mexican in the kitchen and told her that she was going for a walk in the nearby mountains. The woman surprised Lucina by offering her a mare named Luna for the little adventure, telling Lucina that surely it would be safer on horseback than on foot. Canadian women had more trouble fitting into the jungle scenery than Mexican women, explained Señora Labotta. Lucina accepted gratefully, glad that the Mexican seemed to show some concern regarding her safety.

It's a good sign, Lucina thought, as she followed her host to the little barn. *At least she doesn't look like she wants to roast me alive. Yet.*

After having confirmed to Señora Labotta that she had ridden a horse at least a few dozen times in her life, Lucina urged Luna on through the jungle. The day was hot and humid, and she was grateful for having cut her brown hair prior to the trip. Short hair always made her feel lighter and younger. Lucina and Luna traversed a little brook and after a few minutes of riding harmoniously, Lucina felt the strangest urge to talk to the horse.

"Ever since I arrived here 3 days ago," she began, "I have felt that the world here is so alien yet there's this tranquility that I have never felt before in my life. Normally I need my PC to feel good, but now I feel like I need a bit of nature. It's funny because I never really liked nature back in Montreal. Is there nature in Montreal, anyway?"

The mare trotted at a good pace, twitching her ears from time to time, giving the impression that she was listening to Lucina's chatter.

"Spanish is rich and somewhat romantic," Lucina continued, "And here people also seem rich and romantic in a weird way. They don't seem pressed by time and work; rather, it seems they don't really care about work. When I talk with them, they smile most of the time and take their time serving me. I guess their way of life is totally different from what I first imagined."

As Luna stopped to chew on some grass, Lucina gently stroked her gleaming white mane and admired her strong neck. *I have always liked horses more than other animals,* Lucina realized. Perhaps it is because my mother read to me so many times *Gulliver's Travels,* and I heard about the Houyhnhnms and their greater reason so often.

"My life is not that bad, I guess. I'm glad that I program computers rather than sell things, or else I would have killed myself a long time ago. Imagine spending your life chasing people in stores and saying the same things over and over? 'Why, sir, this looks *lovely* on you, just *lovely!*' or 'Madame, you need another television, a bigger one, even if you already have three. It doesn't matter.' Argh, it's so disgusting. At least people chase after me and not the other way around. Yes, Doctor Field told me I have to learn to count my blessings. I guess I am blessed because I don't sell things all day long."

The horse was trotting again at a good pace.

"Señora Labotta is the weirdest person I have ever met. Yet sometimes she says very deep things and I like that. I never hear people talk like her. She told me this morning that I should try to see beyond the shells of humans. That sounds like something coming out of the movie *Ghost in the Shell,* I still have to think about that one. Anyhow, she makes me very nervous sometimes with her intense staring problem, so maybe I'll only stay a few days and then excuse myself and go back to the hotel, I'll see."

Luna was leading the way now. Lucina pulled on the reigns to steer her back in the direction from which they had come. As human and horse slowly turned back, Lucina wrapped up her short monologue.

"Teleo seems like a nice guy, but I am really not looking for anyone right now. Men are only trouble, you know Luna, only trouble. It's always the same story: The want sex and I want intelligent exchanges. Good Lord, it's amazing that men rule when quite obviously the connectionist networks are more developed in us females."

They continued their journey together in silence thereafter. Lucina was filled with a peaceful feeling. Perhaps it was better to talk to a horse than a human because it could never give her advice: It could only listen. Perhaps Lucina needed someone who would listen to her.

*   *   *

By the time Lucina retraced the path back to Señora Labotta's, the sun was already setting. Pink, blue, purple, orange swirls swept across the sky, and at that moment, Lucina felt like a child again, observing the world with new eyes. *Truly, Doctor Field was right about sending me to Oaxaca,* she thought happily as she jumped down from Luna.

"Oaxaca is filled with magic," Doctor Field had said. "All you have to do is sit back and wait for the spell to begin. And bring a hat, so you don't get sunstroke meanwhile."

Up ahead, Lucina spotted open land and saw the lawn behind the Mexican's house. She noticed again what a funny house Señora Labotta lived in, with its dusty little square windows, shaggy porch, yellow peeling paint, white wavering shutters. *This kind of place in Montreal would belong to the nearest bum,* Lucina noted. *Yet the gorgeous flowers give it some charm and the square table with the golden eyes some magical element.*

When Lucina arrived at the stable, she tied Luna up and headed up the uneven stairs of the house. Upon entering, she was amazed to see the cleanliness of the place. Although the living room was no bigger than her bedroom in Montreal, it was neatly organized and everything seemed in its proper place. A single brown couch lay against the wall to the right, a tiny television sat on a high, plain wooden table to the left, and a dim Mexican carpet hung on the wall in front of her. On it was the image of two eagles circling the same tree. The only window in the living room was to the right, above the couch.

"*Buenas tardes,*" called out a male voice from the kitchen to Lucina's left. Teleo appeared in the living room, wiping his hands on a cloth.

"Good evening, Teleo," Lucina replied with a swift smile. "I tied Luna up to the post near the stable."

"*Gracias,* come on in the kitchen, we kept you some quesadillas," he replied, smiling.

The kitchen came into sight with its orange and green walls and its tiny little Mexican hats hanging on the walls. A round oak table stood to her right and around the table were four old-looking wooden chairs. A vase of multi-colored flowers had been placed in the center of the table, giving the kitchen an ever more colorful aspect.

Clearly Mexicans have a different color palette than Canadians, Lucina thought as she settled herself in the seat close to the wall. Teleo brought over a basket of quesadillas and some guacamole and after thanking him, Lucina eagerly ate, realizing that she was famished.

"Excuse me, have you got some sort of meat?" she asked Teleo after a few bites.

He raised his eyebrows.

"Don't you know what Ovid said about meat-eating? That the Golden Age stopped when we started eating meat?"

"Ah no, sorry, I take it you don't eat meat here?"

"No, my mother and I believe that humans can survive without killing other creatures. Most animals sold in stores have been badly treated before being butchered, so their blood is contaminated with fear and suffering, a bad thing to digest. Also, nowadays there are so many chemicals in meat that it's giving people cancer. Do have some beans; they contain a lot of protein, and they're not animals."

Lucina looked at the beans and shrugged. Why not? After having made sure that no one else was going to accompany her, she dug into the food with hunger. The beans were spicy, a little too spicy for her taste buds, so she reached for the glass of water.

Teleo asked her how the stroll had been, if she had enjoyed the sights and the sounds of beautiful Oaxaca valley, and if she had seen any exotic creatures. Lucina admitted that she had never quite enjoyed nature as much as that afternoon in the jungle. Teleo smiled and sat down opposite his guest, watching her as she ate quietly. His presence had a strange, unsettling affect on her. She felt her stomach contract slightly and quickly took several sips of a second glass of water. Through the rectangular kitchen window, she noticed that night was slowly descending on the valley.

"*Mi madre* tells me that you don't like men shells? What a pity!" Teleo said, his eyes bright and piercing. He leaned forward in his chair, brushing a few rebel hairs from his eyes, smiling.

Lucina began to feel the color rising to her cheeks.

"Yes, I seem to have encountered some bad male shells in my life," she answered, trying to repress her embarrassment.

Now I know to watch my mouth around here, she thought angrily.

At that precise moment, Señora Labotta came sauntering into the kitchen as if on cue and sat down at the table next to Lucina. Her long hair was braided on top of her head, making her round cheeks seem even rounder than usual. She nodded to both Teleo and Lucina, and began rolling herself a quesadilla. Lucina noted that she mostly filled it with beans, onions and sour cream.

Teleo laughed and patted his mother on the shoulder.

"So, *mi madre* has been explaining to you her theories on shells and souls," he said with a grin. "Do you consider yourself a lesbian then?"

Lucina felt her face growing hotter still. Señora Labotta turned an attentive ear towards her.

"Pardon me? It's not because I dislike men that I am a lesbian!" Lucina replied, somewhat ruffled. The familiar feeling of defensiveness crept up in her and she bit her lip. Teleo smiled, raising both his hands as a sign of surrender.

"Okay, okay," replied Teleo. "Have you thought of becoming a lesbian?"

"No, I don't think you can just flick your finger and become gay. I think you're either born gay or straight. You can't just become gay, that doesn't happen," Lucina said, avoiding Teleo's serpent eyes. "Anyhow, I never said I hated men shells: I just had really bad experiences with men up to now."

"You think you are born straight or gay?" Señora Labotta said slowly. Lucina nodded her head. *Oh no, here we go, another discussion on sexless realities,* she moaned inwardly. *Is this ever going to stop?*

"I would not say that," continued the woman squinting at Lucina. "I think we are all born bisexual, señorita, and that the world forces us to focus on the opposite shell. Really, we should have no preference. It should be natural to be attracted to both male and female shells. It is not the *shells* which attract us but the *spirits* in the shell."

She paused as she bit into her rather over-stuffed quesadilla.

"You know, in dreams we couple as much with men as with women, if you have not noticed," she said, wiping her mouth with a napkin. "It is very common. We are driven by our sexual impulses in all realms, and within the dream realm our egos cannot interfere and tell us, 'This is bad, this is good' when it comes to sexual attraction."

At that moment, Teleo got up, went to the fridge, and pulled out three cold Sol beers. Lucina gratefully accepted one and drank in silence, still fidgeting in her seat. Sweat had begun to dribble down her forehead and she wiped it away quickly, hoping no one had noticed.

Teleo asked his mother in Spanish to change the subject, pointing out that Lucina was obviously uncomfortable, but Señora Labotta continued as though she hadn't heard him.

"Señorita Lucina, when you were young, did you only play *el doctor* with the boys? Or did you also play with the girls?"

Lucina looked at her and shrugged, unsure of how to reply. The conversation was starting to seriously aggravate her. She had a flash of the quiet room at Posada Margarita and really regretted having left it. She saw the brightly lit bathroom with its rusted taps, the small claustrophobic shower with its broken shower head, the comfortable little bed in the corner.

Teleo coughed loudly. Lucina jolted back into reality.

"Well, señorita, you seemed lost in your thoughts. I hope we haven't offended you in any way," he said, softly fingering the cap of his Sol beer.

Lucina gave him a quick smile.

"Not at all, I'm just not used to hearing such notions," she said, coughing. *I need to get out of here fast,* she thought. *I will feign tiredness, that should do the trick.*

After a few more minutes of innocent conversation, she excused herself from the table, pretending to stifle a yawn. As she walked back to her tent in the windless dark night, she noticed that she was preoccupied by what had been discussed. Could she indeed be bisexual without knowing it? Worse still, could all humans be bisexuals and not know it yet? The notion was very disturbing to Lucina and it took her some time to fall asleep that first night.

Chapter 3

"*Squawk...squawk...Squawk....*"

Slowly, Lucina opened one eye.

"What in the devil is that sound?" she mumbled. With effort, she dragged herself out of the pale blue sleeping bag that Señora Labotta had graciously lent her and peaked out of the tent mosquito screen. A big white bird flew by into the nearby palm trees, letting out another terrific noise. Lucina groaned and fell back unto the thin mattress, feeling stiff all over.

After a few minutes, she wandered out unto the front lawn in her cotton pyjamas. Observing that the sun was just rising over the distant mountains in the East, Lucina deducted that it was probably very early. *What kind of vacation is this anyway?* she lamented inwardly. *I can't even sleep in and I have to listen to some lady talk about shells and lesbians half the day. At least her son isn't that bad.*

Lucina's stomach growled loudly. She got dressed, brushed her short hair, climbed out of her tent, and decided to knock on the front door of the house, lightly, to see if anyone was up. To her surprise, Teleo greeted her, already dressed and looking as fresh as a new-born baby. He explained that his mother had gone into town that morning to work and then asked Lucina if she wanted to shower. Without hesitation, she gladly accepted his offer, following him to the tiny turquoise bathroom located near the kitchen. The mirror to Lucina's left displayed a young brunette woman who looked like she had just survived a hurricane; her hair flew in all directions, her eyes looked puffy and red, and her face looked tired and pale.

I am not looking my best, she noted. *But who cares? I am not trying to get a husband here. I am doing some introspection and that doesn't entail pruning myself for the opposite sex.*

She thanked Teleo. Locking the door behind her, Lucina carefully took off her clothes, placed them on the sink ledge, and placed the towel Teleo had given her on top of her clothes. It had been three days since she had not showered. The shower at Posada Margarita had been cold, and Lucina hated cold showers. Cold water made her feel anxious. As she turned the shower knobs, Lucina smiled as she pictured the warm water soothing her tired skin.

"Arghhh!" she screamed when freezing cold water hit her in the stomach. "Great, just great! How medieval *are* these people?" Angrily, she washed herself and stepped out of the icy cold water. Grabbing the towel, she dried herself, still fuming.

"Lucina, sometimes in life, cold water hits us straight in the face," Doctor Field was saying in her head, "And you have to take it, absorb its nature right into your being. You have to love the cold water. You have to love being cold."

"Shut up, Doctor Field," Lucina snapped.

Doctor Field shut up.

*   *   *

Fifteen minutes later, Lucina walked into the kitchen and to her great dismay, found Teleo beginning his breakfast. He smiled at her and invited her to join him. *This is wonderful,* she thought as she sat down opposite to him. *I hate early morning blabbing, especially if it's going to be about shells and lesbians again.* But to her surprise, Teleo ate in total silence, something

Lucina very much appreciated. *There is a good thing about men,* she thought to herself. *They understand the need for silence in the morning, they understand that most of the time, talk is cheap.*

Lincoln had understood this. They had often spent moments of total silence, just staring into each other's eyes and smiling at one another. Lucina had always liked that about him. It was too bad that she had ended things with him, because he might have been the one.

At the end of breakfast, Teleo asked Lucina if she was interested in seeing the rapids nearby. She felt her stomach tighten at the thought of spending some time alone with him, but since she didn't want to seem rude, after all the kindness he and his mother had shown her, she accepted. Teleo and she got up and they cleaned the dishes in silence. Lucina couldn't help but glance at him occasionally, noticing the smoothness of his arms and hands as he washed the dishes.

After the dishes, they packed a small lunch and stuffed the food into a beige backpack. Lucina went back to the tent to fetch her diary, just in case she wanted to write some thoughts down. They went out to the stable, where Teleo prepared Luna and another horse for the excursion while Lucina busied herself counting the straw bits scattered on the floor of the stable.

"Bueno, vamos en el bosque," Teleo said with enthusiasm as he swung up on his horse. Lucina was less graceful getting into the saddle, but eventually, she was seated comfortably and began a slow trot next to Teleo.

"Do you ride horses up in Canada?" he asked Lucina, giving her a quick look. His black hair fluttered elegantly in the morning air. He wore tight fitting jeans, just the kind that Lucina liked, the ones that flared at the bottom. His simple black t-shirt merged well with his intense dark hair, and for effect or for humour, he reached into his bag and pulled out a cowboy hat. Grinning, he looked at Lucina and put the hat on. "A little American once in a while doesn't kill anyone."

Lucina laughed and decided not to comment.

"Yes, I ride horses in Canada, but not in Montreal, only in the country. I rode a bit when I was younger, but as soon as I moved to Montreal at around ten years old, I gave it up."

Teleo directed his horse around a huge of puddle water and they continued along quietly for a good half hour. The fresh scent of budding flowers greeted them, while birds chirped exotic and enticing songs. All of a sudden, Lucina spotted a long, yellow and red snake curled up in the branches some twenty feet away from where they were. Uncomfortable at the sight of the snake, she turned her attention to the sky and instead observed the fluffy grey clouds. However, the Mexican had noticed the snake as well.

"Most people are afraid of snakes," he said, turning his horse towards Lucina's. "What people don't know is that snakes will bite only as a last resort because they are actually really afraid of humans. I believe that the reason people are afraid of snakes is because deep down, there is a connection between snakes and sexuality. I think that the sight of snakes awakens one's sexuality."

Lucina looked up, curious.

"What people who have read the Bible have failed to understand," Teleo continued, "was that tasting the fruit of the tree of knowledge, was like tasting the fruit of one's inner being, one's sexuality. Sexuality has been taboo for a long time and only now people are realizing how it is truly central to all life. Without the pulse of the snake, the earth would be a fruitless earth. In fact, all seeds arise from the pulse of the snake, be it trees, flowers, animals or humans. People are afraid of snakes if they are afraid of their own sexuality."

"Well, I don't know about snakes, but I do know that all men care about is their own snake, if you know what I mean!" Lucina answered, grinning.

Teleo raised his eyebrows and laughed. Lucina shifted under his gaze.

"Ah, you're right," he said. "There are those who use the snake energy selfishly and blindly and there are those who completely ignore it. That's why many people are confused; either the snake is present but for selfish ends, or it's completely absent. I admit that generally men use it blindly, and most of the time, women repress it. It's sad that humans have forgotten how to use their snake energy."

Lucina sat in the saddle and suddenly felt exposed, naked almost, in front of this tall, curly black haired Mexican. *Why are we talking about snakes and sex?* she thought. *More than that, why are we discussing anything at all when an actual snake is watching us some fifteen feet away?*

Lucina felt jittery and urged Luna on.

"Have no fear, señorita, we're only talking about things. I'm sorry for making you uncomfortable, I can see you don't want to discuss the energy of the snake anymore," Teleo said.

He passed by Lucina and began leading the way towards the rapids once more. After some time, they heard the distinct rush of water and Teleo called out that they should tie the horses up around the big oak trees near the rapids. After tying Luna up, Lucina followed Teleo, prudently searching the ground for any signs of snakes or other dangerous creatures. They came to an opening in the jungle where tall trees lined a narrow river and where tiny red, yellow and brown stones created a colorful carpet on the ground.

Teleo seated himself on the bank of the rapids and closed his eyes while Lucina sat a few feet away from him, taking out her diary. She had neglected it lately, and needed to jot down some things. Looking up at the pale blue sky and feeling content, she began writing.

Dear Diary,   December 5th

I am sitting in front of rapids and thought it would
be good to write some thoughts down. This introspection is taking an odd turn and it's all the fault of Señora Labotta and her smiling, green-eyed son named
Teleo. They have been probing into my sex life and
I feel so damned uncomfortable! We have been discussing sexless reality, lesbians, snakes...I don't know
what will be next. Can you believe that Teleo suggested I might be a lesbian?

Today, Teleo has taken me to see some rapids.
Along the way, we saw a snake and Teleo talked about
our hidden natures. I know I have problems with sex,
but does that man have to keep rubbing my nose in
it? Why doesn't he leave me alone? I still think that
men only want sex and I'm sure he isn't any different.

Señora Labotta told me that I have to go beyond
the shells and see all things, but I don't quite think
I can do that. What exactly does, "seeing all things"
mean anyhow? Isn't there an essence to being a man
and a woman? Isn't that what I was taught? That
women are a certain way, and men a certain way? That
men cheat on their wives, and women back-stab each
other? That men like to screw, and women like to talk?
That men are independent and women dependent?

"Señorita Lucina?"
Lucina quickly turned to look at her companion.
"Would you like to join me?"
"Sure, one minute," she answered, closing her journal and
putting it into her little backpack. She moved a bit closer to
Teleo and he turned to face her. Lucina imitated his sitting

position, placing her legs Indian style and straightening her back.

"Tell me, why did you come to Oaxaca?" Teleo began softly, his eyes semi-closed.

"I came because I needed to take a big break from my life," Lucina replied, staring at the moving waters.

"Señorita..."

"Please Teleo, call me by my name, Luci."

"Okay, Luci. My mother told me that you had a bad experience with your boss. I'm sorry to hear that. Is this why you hate men?"

Lucina quickly looked into his eyes and glanced away.

Doctor Field's voice echoed in her head again; "Follow your instincts instead of your fears. Your instincts are usually right. If you want to say something, say it instead of churning it over and over."

Lucina sighed and replied that she had started hating men at the early age of fifteen. Men had ruined her soul, she told Teleo, and there was nothing to be done about it except try to forget about the past. She looked at the deep blue water whirling by them, hit by a wave of sadness as she recalled the past. Teleo was silent for a few minutes, respecting Lucina's moment of meditation.

"Luci, you know that life is one big test?" he murmured. "It's a test to see if you will fall into the pit of fear, or if you will climb the mountain of love. To climb is harder than to fall."

Lucina stared down at her hands and felt them trembling slightly. His words penetrated deep into her being and she suddenly felt like she wanted to run far away from the charming Mexican man sitting a few feet away from her. She tried to avert his radiant eyes. For the first time since she had arrived in Oaxaca, she felt her guard dropping and heard a familiar voice screaming at her not to let her walls down, but Lucina pushed the voice away.

"The mountain is a wonderful place, yet it takes courage to climb," continued Teleo. "You need to make time for it and you need to be in shape. You must be aware that years can go by before you reach the top. Once you reach it, you see the most beautiful thing; you see the world, you see the sky, and you see everything. Love is everything."

"Yep," Lucina answered somewhat sarcastically, feeling her old self again. "So I take it you're in love?"

His eyes became sad and he quickly looked up at the sky.

"I once knew a woman. I thought she was my soul mate. She was a beautiful woman..." his voice trailed off. Lucina shifted uneasily. "She and I were engaged to be married. One day, a man came and took Patricia's heart away and she married him instead. For a long time, I was very angry at that man and wanted to kill him. In the end, my mother helped me to forget about my anger and made me remember that we can't control love. She even promised me that one day, I would meet my real soul mate."

Lucina asked him why he believed in soul mates when the woman he had loved had left him for another man. Teleo remained silent for some time, and then said softly that he believed in soul mates because he had always felt the presence of a woman near him in his most lonesome moments. Jokingly, she pointed out that maybe what he was feeling was the Virgin Mary consoling him after his loss. Teleo didn't laugh. *Be serious*, Lucina, she told herself. *He is not joking so try to be serious.*

His eyes rested on Lucina again.

"Believe what you want to believe and it will happen to you. Believe that you will love, and you will. Believe that you will live forever, and you will. Belief makes the world turn round."

Somewhat uncomfortable again, Lucina threw a stone

into the tumultuous waters and watched it disappear into the swirling darkness.

Some time later, Teleo handed Lucina bread and cheese from the lunch bag, and they munched on the good food while looking around at the calm scenery. Once in a while, the horses stomped their hooves or threw their heads back, as if wanting attention. When Lucina and Teleo finished their light snack, they gathered their few belongings, saluted the waters, and regained their seats on the horses. Lucina let herself sway from side to side as Luna followed Teleo's horse. Her body felt relaxed that morning with Teleo.

"Bodies are like machines," Doctor Field had once said to Lucina after the burn-out. "If you think your body won't eventually break down when you apply a lot of pressure to it, you are stupid. Why do so many people have cancer? Because they think they can work their bodies and never feel repercussions. People are blind fools. I keep telling them, stop, relax, oil your machine, take a vacation, do what you like…But then they come to me and they are burnt-out. Humans never learn until it's too late, until they're at the limits of death."

Lucina had always thought her body would survive anything, but it had caved in. She remembered her mother's disbelief when she had told her that she was having a burn-out. Her mother had ranted over the phone that burn-outs were for older people, not younger ones, and that young people had no idea what work was, that vacations were for people who had been working for years at the same job. It had been useless trying to explain to her mother that with today's pressures, work schedules and lack of vacations, many younger people were burning-out. Lucina knew all this because Doctor Field had told her that more than half of his clients were under the age of thirty and suffering from severe cases of depressions, burn-outs and psychological illnesses.

"Bodies are fragile, but people don't care. They think that they are gods. If they were gods, there wouldn't be a line-up outside my office every morning," Doctor Field had scoffed.

Teleo turned around and asked Lucina if she was all right. She nodded her head and stared at the thick jungle around them, feeling serene and calm for the first time in a long while.

*   *   *

An hour or so later, they arrived at the Labotta residence, un-saddled the horses, gave them fresh oats, and groomed them. Lucina felt the urge to call her best friend, Stacy. She hadn't called her since the arrival, wondered if they had a phone, and thought of asking Teleo.

"Teleo, do you think it's possible to make a call to Canada from your house? I'll pay the charge of course," Lucina asked quickly.

"No problema, por supuesto. The phone is in the living room, next to the couch. Don't worry about the cost. I'll join you soon," he responded, continuing to brush the horses.

After thanking him, Lucina jogged to the house, and in a few more steps, she was standing in the living room, dialling Stacey's number. It rang four times before her friend picked up.

"Stacey! It's Luci! How are you?"

"Omigod, Luci?" she cried out happily. "I've wanted to hear from you in over four days! How the hell are you?"

"Good, good, everything went well with the flight, and the bus. Now I'm in Oaxaca, staying with two Mexicans..."

"Whaaaat? Are you serious?"

Lucina knew that her best friend would never believe her story, but she told her about the meeting with the strange Mexican woman anyhow, and told her about the camping arrangements as well as the exchange she had made with the stranger. When Lucina told Stacey about the meeting with Teleo, Stacey became excited. Lucina quickly changed the subject, spoke about the quietness of the nature around her, and the slow progress she was making with her introspection. But her friend wanted to hear only about Teleo.

At that moment, the man himself walked into the living room, forcing Lucina to change subjects. She asked Stacey to keep the newspaper clippings of all the latest computer programming jobs in Montreal, then she told her one last time not to worry about her and especially not to mention anything to her mother. Stacey laughed and promised that her secret would be safe.

Lucina hung up the phone quietly and turned to face Teleo. He sat himself in the couch with a beer in hand and wiped the sweat off his forehead. It unexpectedly became humid in the living room.

"So, Luci, tell me about Montreal," he said, indicating for her to sit down. She sat down on the couch, making sure to keep a safe distance of three feet between them on the couch.

"Ah, Montreal is a place like no other," she began, happy that they were not talking about sex anymore. "There are many diverse ethnicities, so everyone feels at home. We have a China town, and an Italian town. Everyone says that Montreal is a very welcoming place, and I totally agree because I have never felt such warmth from any other city. On top of it, it's a very safe place; we don't have that much crime at all."

Teleo nodded, taking a long sip of his beer.

"What do you do for a living there?" he asked.

Without going into details too much, she told him that she had been working in computers for four years and that it was something that she enjoyed, most of the time. When Teleo asked her why she had chosen computers, Lucina paused, trying to think of the most honest thing to say. After a few seconds of thinking, she admitted that computers were easier to understand than humans and that they didn't complain as much. Computers were objects that simplified life and made life more interesting.

There was a pause as Teleo studied Lucina's face.

"You think a computer has more meaning than a human being?"

Lucina looked down at her hands. *Oh no*, she thought. *Here it comes: The questioning. When will it stop? Do I have to answer all these questions all the time?*

"Well, I can't say computers have more *meaning*, really," Lucina replied, searching for her words carefully. "I think they just keep me occupied and busy. Anyway, people are so complicated. I don't really have the patience for people, you know?"

Lucina's mind flashed back to her last meeting with Doctor Field. He had been sitting watching her with his bright black eyes and had blurted out to her to get a life.

"What do you mean?" she had responded, offended.

"I mean, get a life. Computers are not living things, they are dead things. They keep us busy but a human challenges us, a human being confronts us with who we really are. A human being has a *soul*. Computers just help pass the time until we die. They drain our vital energy until we are all shrivelled up inside. Get a life. Go out and dance. Drink. Get drunk. Meet new people. Have sex for Chris's sake. Sex is good for vital energy."

Needless to say, that last meeting had ended abruptly. Lucina had said that she was feeling ill and that she wanted to end therapy then and there. Doctor Field had nodded.

"I understand the wiring," Lucina continued, looking at Teleo. "I don't understand humans at all. I can program computers, but can't program humans."

Teleo sympathized with Lucina, but pointed out that

computers created holes for people to live in; holes could block out the sun, holes could make people forget that life was made to be shared. He stated that like Aristotle, he believed humans were social beings, and that without other people, humans could easily lose their footing in the world. When Patricia left, he explained, he had dug himself a hole of anger and had stayed there, guarding it like a watch dog. Anyone trying to get in would get something blown off. Lucina asked him how he had managed to climb out of his hole and Teleo answered that he had just become sick and tired of staying there. The sun had been lacking in his life, and he had needed fresh air.

Impulsively, Lucina got up because the talk was getting to her. She was starting to feel depressed, and so excused herself, telling Teleo that she wanted to spend some time alone for the rest of the day. Teleo nodded and told her that he totally understood. He had errands to run for his mother anyhow, he explained.

Lucina went back to her tent, glad to be away from the incessant questions, and took out her diary for the second time that day. She felt that she had so many thoughts whirling around in her head that she needed to straighten out her head a little through writing. Lying back on her sleeping bag, she made sure all the screens were opened so as to let the little bit of refreshing wind come in, and began to write where she had left off at the rapids.

> It seems to me as though the more I'm here in Oaxaca, the more I feel lost. I thought before that I knew where I was going in life. I always thought that I could spend my life with computers, and make some good money. Now that I think about it, maybe Teleo is right: Maybe I am living in a hole, a hole of numbers and wires.

What is the meaning of this life? I feel as though
I am useless. Before at NewI I felt somewhat special
and people talked to me, even if they were sexist. Now
I feel like I have no place to go, nothing to do. I really feel useless. I remember that when I was a child,
I wanted to be a writer. I don't know what happened
to that.

Teleo asked me how Montreal was. I didn't tell
him everything. The truth is, I really don't feel at
home there. I don't know where "home" is, but it's not
in that city. I'm annoyed by it. Everything pisses me
off; the people, the energy which once was good, the
cars, the dirty sidewalks...I don't really feel like going
back there at all, now that I think about it. What is
waiting for me there now? Stacey and mom, and a few
random faces I see once every six months...Why am I
living there at all?

Maybe I should move to another country.

Sighing, Lucina put her pen down and rubbed her eyes. *This
journal is getting more depressing by the minute,* she groaned
inwardly. *Maybe I should just take an afternoon siesta and then
eat supper.* Closing her eyes and curling up on top of her soft
sleeping bag, Lucina soon fell asleep.

She had a very strange dream. In the dream, she was
standing in the middle of a forest and birds were chirping all
around her. Bright sunlight created long black shadows on the
green ground, there was a humid feel to the place, and moss,
ferns and colorful flowers grew all around her. Looking down,
she noticed that she was wearing a medieval white garment
that looked like a nightdress. Slowly, Lucina began to walk
through the forest and soon reached a little hole cut into a
huge, old oak tree.

An elf emerged from within the tree and took her hand. He brought Lucina inside the tree and made her sit down on a small, awkward stool. He sat in front of her and began talking to her about soul mates. In a whispered voice, he told her that soul mates could be found just by believing in love itself, and believing in how love heals all things. He explained to her that finding a soul mate was not as difficult as she believed, and that it was just a matter of picturing meeting a mirror.

"One has to look long and hard in this mirror and not flinch. Your soul mate will speak to you, make you feel like you want to run away all the time. Like your own reflection, he will show you the truth, he will show you your tears, your laughter, your sadness. He will help you to reach enlightenment if you want to. Your soul mate is a true guide in your life; with him you can reach high peaks and never feel alone."

Lucina felt irritated and wanted to push the elf away. His words didn't make any sense to her; she didn't believe in soul mates, so why was an elf talking to her about this anyway?

"I know you don't believe in soul mates, but trust me, they exist," the elf continued, "And sometimes you have more than one. Sometimes, when a person really wants to evolve, she can meet a few soul mates in the same life. They are all there as powerful mirrors. Learn to believe in mirrors, they will shine the way."

All of a sudden, the scenery completely changed. Lucina found herself in a hall filled with large mirrors. The ceiling was very high, the light was scarce, and there was a smell of newly varnished wood in the air. There came a rush of wind behind her which pushed her towards a long, wooden table with many antique-looking wooden chairs around it. Lucina saw that one chair had her name on it, and ever so carefully, she sat down in it, looking around her with interest.

No other being was in sight.

Unexpectedly, she felt someone's warm hand on her right hand. It caressed her fingers one by one, until it came to the center of her hand. Then, she felt a bolt of fire run through her body. Frightened, she wanted to pull back, but the voice of the elf came back and said again; "Your soul mate is a true guide in your life; with him you can reach high peaks and never feel alone."

Lucina woke up in a jump and right away looked wildly about her, as though expecting to see the elf. Concluding that there was no one other than her in the tent, she sighed and rubbed her eyes for a few seconds.

"How dreams are so vivid sometimes!" she mumbled as she unzipped the tent and stretched outside. To her surprise, it was already dusk and the sun was disappearing behind the mountains. Lucina's dream vanished from her consciousness as soon as she stepped out into the real world.

As she came closer to the house, she noticed the light on in the kitchen and started to feel edgy about seeing Señora Labotta again. She hadn't seen her all day and was beginning to feel as though she should have done some yard work instead of sleeping. Lucina walked into the orange and green brightly lit kitchen, and saw Señora Labotta, sitting in one of the chairs, staring intensely into her tea cup. The look on her face told her that something was not quite right. She greeted the woman quietly and then asked her if anything was wrong.

"*Si*, señora. I have to leave town for a few days. My father has fallen and broken his hip, I must go and visit him," she said quietly. "I felt it that something would happen to him, and that I should have left earlier. The doctors in Mexico tell me that he will be fine, but I must go and see him. I leave you in the care of Teleo; he is a skilled healer, in case you suffer from any discomfort while I am away."

Lucina expressed her sympathies and asked Señora Labotta if there were things that she could do around the house while she was away. The woman answered that Teleo would take care of everything for her, but that Lucina could continue weeding the back until her return. Then, she excused herself and said she would be leaving that night on the next bus to Mexico City. With troubled eyes, she left the kitchen and told Lucina to enjoy supper.

After thanking her host and wishing her the best, Lucina nibbled on some fresh vegetables and dip that Señora Labotta had graciously prepared for her, wondering where Teleo was. As soon as the thought hit her, he appeared in the entrance of the house and spoke a few quick words in Spanish to his mother. They hugged, and Señora Labotta waved good-bye to both of them.

She is a lightening packer, Lucina noticed. *Those suitcases appeared out of nowhere it seems.*

Teleo walked into the kitchen and sat himself opposite to Lucina.

"I think that everything will be all right," he said, as he took a bite of a celery stick. "My mother gets worried whenever someone falls ill. She's afraid that they'll die before she sees them."

Lucina expressed her sympathies again and offered her help if he needed it. He thanked her, handed her a plate, and told her to begin eating. Supper that night consisted of raw vegetables, rice and bread. Teleo explained during the meal that he and his mother were strong believers in eating raw food. The body absorbed more of the nutrients, he pointed out, and eating raw was much better for the liver in the long run. The liver was tired of digesting nasty hydrogenated oils.

Together they cleaned the dishes after supper and then Lucina told Teleo that she was tired and wanted to go to bed early that night. He nodded, seemed somewhat disappointed, but didn't press her for explanations.

"Tomorrow I will weed," she told him. He smiled and answered that he didn't doubt her integrity as a weeder.

Lucina had no more strange dreams that night, to her great relief.

Chapter 4

The next morning, Teleo cooked breakfast and they ate on the porch, listening to the sounds of nature waking up around them. Lucina thanked him repeatedly for his tasty food and Teleo just smiled, saying it was only natural to cook for such a charming guest. Lucina avoided his eyes and looked up at the porch roof. Teleo noticed that she was studying the nests and told her about the different birds nesting beneath their roof, explaining how most of the birds stayed long enough to have a few young ones and then they would fly off magically.

At the end of breakfast, Teleo suggested that he take his guest to the Monte Albán ruins 10 kilometers from the city that day. Lucina thought it was a wonderful idea, and since she had never seen any ruins before in her life, she agreed to go without a second thought. They packed a light lunch of sandwiches, prepared some water bottles, and quickly got dressed for the excursion. By 8 a.m., Teleo and Lucina were on a Greyhound bus headed towards Monte Albán.

The bus dropped the two adventurers off in the middle of nowhere. They walked in silence to the site and half an hour later, paid an entrance fee of 10 American dollars, and began the tour of the beautiful ancient Zapotec site.

"This is one of the most ancient cities of the Mesoamerican cultures," Teleo explained as they began the tour. "Humans first occupied this valley around 8000 before Christ, but it wasn't until 700 before Christ that the city began to take on a political role in Oaxaca. The apex of the city was in the years 300 to 750 after Christ. During this period, around 35,000 people lived in Monte Albán. After 750, no one knows for sure why, but the city was abandoned and became a ceremonial center more than a city."

"So you're also a historian?" Lucina commented with a grin.

Teleo shrugged casually, but a discreet smile played on his lips. They walked side by side down the main path of the site. Lucina stood in awe when they fell upon the first, large stone buildings. The ruins looked impressive in the early morning sun, as though they wanted the tourists to remember their power in ancient times. Happily, Lucina noted that there were very few tourists around at that hour. She wanted to be alone with the stones, wanted them to carry her back to their world, far away from hers.

"In school, ancient Mesoamerican civilizations really interested me," Teleo responded, walking slowly next to Lucina. They walked past a slanted, crooked pyramid with a few eroding stairs.

"I was always curious. What is the difference between the Mayans, the Olmecs, the Toltecs, and this civilization, the Zapotecs?" Lucina asked him, glad to be learning something new, and very relieved not to be talking about lesbians, snakes or shells anymore.

As they continued their slow walk around the many beautiful, magical ruins, Teleo explained that the Olmecs were a mysterious race of artists, who mainly lived from 1200 to 300 B.C. They sculpted many jaguar figures, because the jaguar was their prominent symbol of strength, cunningness and endurance. The Olmecs also sculpted huge stone heads, which some believed to be the figures of lords and kings. Teleo pointed out that the Olmecs were most probably the first ones who cre-

ated the famous ball game, as well as the first to perform human sacrifices. Also, they used math and calendars, much like
the Mayans later. The decline of their culture was mysterious:
No one knew for sure why their cities had been abandoned.

"After the Olmecs came the Mayans. Some say that the
Mayans started to appear around 1000 B.C., thus during the
same time as the Olmecs. The Mayans are known for their
cities which were built in rain forests, notably Palenque, Tikal
and Chichen Itza. The rain forest surroundings made it hard
to cultivate food, and this is one of the reasons the Mayan
civilizations abandoned their cities after 900 A.D."

"The Mayans believed that the world was divided into
three parts: The underworld, the earth and the sky. A tree
called the *Wacah Chan* linked the three realms together. Un-
like our notion of linear time, time was cyclical for Mayans
and the present depended a lot on knowing the past cycles
of time. The Mayans had more than one calendar, and the
two most important ones were the 260 day calendar called the
Tzolkin and the 365 day calendar called the *Haab*. A very important aspect of Mayan life was blood-letting; Mayan kings
and queens needed to draw their own blood during ceremo-
nies, and to do this they would pass sharp ropes or objects
through their tongues or genitals as an offering to their gods."

Lucina couldn't help but shudder when Teleo mentioned
this. He laughed, and assured her that today, Mayans did not
perform such rituals anymore.

"What is really amazing about the Mayans is that they
had very bizarre notions of beauty," he continued, as they
stopped to look at a temple near the center of the site. "They
believed that being cross-eyed was very attractive, so they
would dangle objects in front of their children's eyes to make
them cross-eyed. This practice is still going on today. Mayans
also found large, slopping foreheads attractive, so they used

to bind their children's foreheads with long boards to achieve this look."

Teleo interrupted his history account to explain to Lucina that they were now approaching *Los Danzantes,* or the dancers. He pointed out that these stone sculptures had an Olmec look to them, and that the figures might have been sacrificial victims, since they were nude women. They continued to walk around the three middle buildings, which certainly did not look like an astronomical observatory, as Teleo noted.

"And who came after the Mayans?" Lucina probed him, as they sat down on the steps of one of the smaller buildings. Teleo took out a water bottle and offered her a drink. Lucina accepted, and turned to watch him, noticing how his eyes glittered with enthusiasm.

"The civilization known as the Toltecs came after. They lived from around the 9th to the 12th century after Christ. They are known notably for their city Tula, which has beautiful carved warrior figures all along its walls. They were warriors who expanded their kingdom quite a bit during their time, and they conquered many Mayan cities. The Toltecs believed that Quetzacoatl, a warrior god and the creator of humanity, would return to their city one day. It is believed that the Chichimecs destroyed the Toltecs around 1200 A.D."

Lucina noticed how when Teleo spoke, his jaw became more firm, as though he were filled with godly confidence. She pictured him giving a lecture in a university, and imagined how all the women would stare at him in fascination and admiration. *Would he notice me in the crowd of beautiful university students?* she pondered. *Probably not. He would be too busy fighting off the thousands of beautiful women trying to get his attention.*

"The term Toltec has also been used by several famous writers, Carlos Castaneda and Don Miguel Ruiz to name a few, to signify a person who has a great awareness and knowledge of the world," Teleo added, interrupting Lucina's wandering thoughts. She was surprised to hear that writer's name again. Hadn't Señora Labotta mentioned Castaneda in her store a few days ago? Lucina mentioned her observation to Teleo. He smiled and said that Castaneda was his mother's favorite author.

"The Aztecs lived in the 13th, 14th and 15th centuries A.D," Teleo continued, distractedly picking blades of grass around the steps they were sitting on. "They were a ferocious warrior people who practiced a great deal of human sacrifice. Their capital was named Tenochtitlan. In this same city, it is reputed that they sacrificed more than 84,000 people in the period of four days, but whether this is true or not is debatable. One of the reasons the Aztecs sacrificed so many people is that they believed that the world was in constant opposition, and that humans could somewhat control this constant opposition through human sacrifice, thus hoping to achieve a better balance between creation and destruction."

"Furthermore, the Aztecs are also known for their complex political systems. They had many laws, which often resulted in death. When Hernán Cortés arrived in Oaxaca in 1519, he was appalled at such a barbaric practice as human sacrifice. As soon as the Spaniards arrived, Tenochtitlan fell. It seems that Cortés was himself a practitioner of another type of barbarism."

"So Cortés killed those people because they were too barbaric?" Lucina asked Teleo as they got up again. "Isn't that ironic somehow?" Teleo nodded. He replied that what any white man did was never considered barbaric, at least not in the history books.

"Come, let's take a look at this building. We have a magnificent view of the whole site from there," Teleo urged as they climbed one of the last buildings. When Teleo and Lucina reached the top, Lucina was out of breath, but the view was worth every step of the way. From where they were standing, they could see the Oaxaca valley very well. Teleo mentioned that they were 2000 feet above Oaxaca City.

Lucina closed her eyes and felt planets away from her old life.

Because the sun was starting to get hotter, Lucina suggested to Teleo that they find some shade to eat their lunch, so they descended the temple steps and found a secluded area, far from the arriving tourists. Lucina sat in the soft grass, observing how Teleo slowly and elegantly settled down on the ground. He handed her a cheese sandwich and took out a salad for himself. She rested her back against a large banyan tree and looked up at the clear baby blue sky.

"Lucina," Teleo said, as he turned to look at her.

"Yes?" she said, nearly choking on her sandwich.

"You have a funny soul, has anyone ever told you that?"

"Umm, no, but I hope that's a compliment?" she said, somewhat uneasy.

Teleo laughed, and gave her a warm look. Lucina laughed, unsure of why she was laughing.

*   *   *

They arrived back home late afternoon. Lucina would have slept on the bus coming back, had it not been for the terrible road with the huge pot holes. *Now there is something Mexico and Quebec have in common*, she realized: *Pot holes.*

When they arrived at the house, Teleo excused himself and said he had chores to do. Lucina answered that she also had things to do, even if she didn't really. She wanted to seem independent, so she went back to her tent, took out her diary, and sat down on the sleeping bag.

Dear Diary,   December 6th

What a beautiful day I had today. Teleo took me to
the Monte Albán site. I saw wonderful, ancient stone
buildings. We went early so as to beat the tourists and
it was worth it. I got a free history lesson on ancient
Mesoamerican civilizations.

   I had no idea that Teleo knew so many things.

   I couldn't help but notice his eyes today while
he talked. He has such intense, green eyes that I had
trouble focusing on what he was saying to me. On the
bus coming home, I tried to avoid his eyes by looking
out the window the whole time. In reality, I can't bear
to look at him too long. I have this nervous feeling
when I do and it only indicates trouble if you ask me.

   A few weeks ago, I am certain I would have liked
to be one of the sacrificed victims on a Mayan altar,
but now, it seems strange: I have this sudden desire
to live.

Lucina put her journal away, curled up in a ball, and took
a late afternoon nap. No strange dreams disturbed her that
afternoon. When she awoke some time later, her stomach
was growling with hunger. She wandered lazily back to the
house, and stopped short when she caught sight of Teleo in
the kitchen.

   He was busy mopping the kitchen floor.

   This man is obviously a prime example of the opposite sex, she
thought as she watched him mop with grace and efficiency.
His hair dipped in his face like tiny black ringlets attached to
springs, and it seemed as though he were performing a mys-
tical dance of some sort while mopping. His legs were in a

strange spread-eagle position and while mopping, he would execute a 180 degree turn with the mop in hand. She caught a glimpse of a muscular thigh as he dipped back around.

"*Hola*, Luci!" he said with a jump, as he nearly collided into her. He wiped his hands on his jeans and dropped the mop into his red bucket.

"*Hola!*" she replied, looking at the mop instead of him. "Can I help you with anything?"

"No, *por favor*. You can sit down and relax. Oh, by the way, we're having a little fiesta later, I hope you don't mind?"

"Not at all," she answered, alarmed.

On no, people were coming. That meant she had to try to look presentable. She quietly snuck back to the tent and looked through her suitcase for something somewhat attractive to wear, but the choice was very limited. After several minutes of deliberation, Lucina pulled out a faded brown leather skirt and a blue silk blouse. Nodding in approval, she carried her things to the house and walked into the turquoise bathroom.

I need a shower and a good shampoo before the guests arrive, she mused. As she looked at herself in the mirror of the tiny bathroom, she noticed how tanned she had become over the past few days. It was certainly a change from the pale, white winter skin she was so used to seeing in the mirror back home.

After a cold shower, Lucina combed her hair, and looked around for some hair gel but of course, she found nothing except some weird herbal mixture in a blue bottle with the words *Lavendula* written on it. Sighing, she decided to leave her hair the way it was.

Lucina jumped at the sound of a loud knock on the front door. She had never liked parties. Nervously, she glanced at her reflection in the small cracked mirror once more and took a deep breath. It had been a long time since she had been to a party. The last party she had been to, had been a catastrophe. She had sat on a couch for three hours, staring at the dozens of paintings on the wall, trying to figure out what her purpose in life was while her friend had shamelessly flirted with a stranger from Paris.

"What's wrong with you, Luci? Why don't you go and talk to that tall business man over there?" her friend had shot out, when the stranger had gone to the washroom.

"I don't think men are worth the effort," Lucina had replied, trying to look as though she was enjoying herself. Her friend had shrugged.

It had been a long night.

But Lucina had learned a lot from human interaction that night. For example, she had noticed how when people are attracted to each other, they spend their time smiling like fools and chattering like idiots. She hoped she never would look like her friend that night, smiling so hard that her eyes looked like tiny dots on her face.

Lucina walked out of the little bathroom and noticed immediately the tall, long-haired aged man standing near Teleo. The man looked up at Lucina directly, smiling warmly. The man must have been around fifty, was wearing brown faded jeans, a simple black t-shirt, and a vest of purple, blue, red, orange and many more colors. Lucina realized at last that she was looking at a Mayan vest, a very colorful Mayan vest. His grey hair was neatly braided at the back in one long braid, beads were scattered in his hair, and in his right hand he held what looked like a flat Indian drum. In his left hand, he carried a huge tequila bottle.

"*Hola*, señorita! *Me llamo Kailo. Como está?*" asked the man with a huge grin.

Lucina groaned inwardly. What kind of party were they going to have? She replied politely that she was fine, thank you. Teleo laughed, they exchanged more words in Spanish, and eventually, the older man turned around and introduced his wife, Kaila. She was dressed in a vibrant dress of the same colors as her husband's vest and had greyer hair, piled up in a knot on the top of her head. Kaila looked at Lucina, smiled briefly, and then turned her attention to Teleo again.

Lucina couldn't help but feel the alienation settling in.

Kaila and Kailo? Where had they picked out their names, Walmart?

Teleo seemed really happy to see them and suggested that they should start the fire. Lucina expected more people to come, but when no one else showed up, she concluded that Mexicans had a different meaning of the word "fiesta" than Canadians.

They built a fire in the backyard and a few minutes later, Teleo carried over the old plastic chairs from the porch. Lucina chose a chair in between Teleo and the older man while Teleo sparked the fire, quietly watching as the flames began to take life. The song "Firestarter" came to mind as soon as Teleo bent down and blew on the flames. Grinning inwardly, Lucina tried to picture Teleo at a rave, dancing to Prodigy. Somehow the two didn't quite fit.

Kaila was a very quiet woman. She mostly stared at the fire and didn't look like she wanted to talk, but her husband was the opposite. He spent an hour or so chattering away in broken English to Lucina, asking her a ton of questions concerning Canada. Did they have igloos up there? Did they eat caribou meat every day? Did they shoot their own animals? Did they have cars or horses? Did they have a thing called internet there? Did they own houses, or work for people who owned houses? Did they make their own clothes, or did they buy them? Did they have summer at all? Did they grow their own food, or go to the supermarket?

Lucina could tell Kailo wasn't a very educated man, so she decided to be patient with him. She explained to him the basics of living in Canada, stressing that although some Eskimos still lived in igloos, Canadians had moved on to better and more sophisticated ways of living. She explained that they most definitely had internet, and that she was in the computer business.

"*Mama mía!*" Kailo cried out excitedly. "We have computer expert with us today. How lovely. I need buy computer very soon, you recommend something good?"

Lucina recommended him PCs, knowing full well he had no idea what a PC was.

In a friendly sign of affection the man offered her some tequila and without any hesitation, she accepted a glass. It was so warm and lovely that Lucina drank it down reasonably fast.

"Luci, Kailo is the village healer. He is the man who trained me to be a healer," Teleo said, as he winked at the older man. The older man started coughing violently, and then stopped to look at Lucina with a serious face.

"*Sabes*, señorita, *con este* man here, woman safe all life. He know all trades of herbs...learn from me!" Kailo said, and then burst into squeals of laughter.

Lucina glanced at Teleo out of the corner of her eye, surprised to hear that he was not only a historian but also a doctor. That was impressive. *Perhaps he looks so healthy because he is a doctor*, she wondered to herself. She questioned Teleo about his profession, but Teleo waved his hand in the air, saying that he was just an ordinary guy helping others.

Throughout the night, they continued to talk, drink tequila, and laugh about random things. Then, Kailo and Kaila started to drum. At first, the sound seemed loud, scattered and inharmonious to Lucina's ears, yet as time went by, she started to notice the complexities of the patterns and variations of force of the two drums. She looked at Kaila, observing how Kaila was leading the sound with her strong, quick hand movements against the drum while Kailo filled in the gaps with his fingers, occasionally pounding a loud bass sound. The music soon became one with the fire, and before long, whether it was the glasses of tequila going down rapidly or simply the night, Lucina suddenly felt like dancing around the fire.

Somewhat drunk by then, she let herself follow the beat of the drums. It was the first time she had danced around a fire in front of perfect strangers. The feeling was truly wonderful. She glimpsed her feet patting the dry ground, saw the flames following the flow of the tribal music, and heard Spanish rising into the dark, midnight air. Laughing, Teleo put his glass of tequila down and without any trouble, he started to follow Lucina around the fire, sometimes singing softly, sometimes singing loudly in Spanish. Lucina started to feel miles away from her old self.

Euphoria hit her little by little. How light and free she felt at that moment, dancing around the fire with the older couple drumming away to various rhythms. Teleo came near her a few times, and she felt the wind move around her as he went by. When he accidentally bumped into her, Lucina couldn't help but feel a warmth rushing through her, a warmth she had rarely felt before that night. She caught glimpses of his muscles flinching as he performed rapid arm movements. He could have easily passed as a true Indian, dancing to the spirits of the earth.

What is happening to me? she thought, alarmed that she was starting to feel so free and light-headed. The past vanished, Canada and its entire stressed-out people disappeared, her mother's incessant religious advice dissipated, Stacey no longer existed, and computers and their humming sounds melted away.

"Luci, for a woman involved with machines, you sure know how to make your body move," commented Teleo softly, as he moved past Lucina. She noticed that he wasn't out of breath.

"Well, I used to watch 'Dirty Dancing' a lot when I was a kid," she replied, stopping to catch her breath. She put her hands on her knees and tried to catch some air. Her lungs felt like they were on fire.

"What is this 'Dirty Dancing'?" he said, with a grin on his face.

She looked up at him, realizing that he was directly flirting with her for the first time. She didn't know what to reply, so she took another swig of her tequila and got up the courage to continue dancing. That was Lucina's way of dealing with great obstacles: She tried to avoid them or ignore them altogether.

They danced some more around the fire, and at last, after about half an hour of dancing, Lucina collapsed in a chair, giggling with dizziness. It was strange how now Mexicans seemed quite normal to her. There she was, surrounded by strangers, feeling every bit at home and happy. She glanced at Kaila, who seemed utterly lost in the rhythm of her drum.

"Señorita Lucina," Kailo said loudly. "You certainly not dance like white woman!"

Lucina's face turned red under the gaze of Teleo and Kailo, and even though her head was spinning, she was still quite conscious of what had been said and she giggled nervously. Teleo threw another few logs in the fire and busied himself with brushing the thick mud off his black boots with his hands. Their eyes locked for a few seconds, but then Lucina looked up at the sky, observing the shimmering stars and the moon.

Out of nowhere, the strange dream came back to Lucina and she thought she saw the elf amidst the stars, saying, "One has to look long and hard in this mirror and not flinch."

Lucina shook her head a few times as she reached for her tequila glass to drown the image of the pesky elf.

*   *   *

Some time later, Lucina had the urge to relieve her bladder, but instead of going to the bathroom, she opted for the nearest hidden shrubs. Teleo called after her to be careful and not to stray too far from the path. Waving to show that she had understood him, Lucina made her way in the dark to the nearest hidden place, and was all of a sudden overwhelmed by nausea. Gradually, this feeling increased and she was forced to crouch on the ground, holding her stomach. The vomit crawled up her throat and splattered on the ground.

Wiping her mouth with her hand, she began searching tentatively for leaves of some kind on which she could wipe herself more thoroughly. She had no desire to go back to the happy campers and let them know that she couldn't hold her liquor, it would reflect terribly on the Canadian culture. As she passed her hand over the moist ground, Lucina felt something slimy on the ground; it was long, thin and was moving slightly. Still rather nauseous and weak, she pressed her hand down on it and realized that she was holding something very much alive, something that was slithering and wet.

"Arghhhh!" Lucina screamed in horror, as the realization hit her that it was a snake.

With all the might she had, she scrambled up and started to run, but she did not get very far; the snake bit her left ankle and it felt as though a knife had gone through her. Lucina tried to kick at it, but her nausea intensified. Darkness slowly caved in on her, fear flashed before her eyes, and a thought burst into her mind; "You are going to die here in Oaxaca."

It wasn't long before Kailo, Teleo and Kaila came into view.

Teleo waved a flashlight in Lucina's face, and loudly said, "*Madre mía! Como es possible? Jesus!*". Kneeling down next to her, he took her up in his strong arms all the while speaking rapidly to Kailo and Kaila in Spanish. He gave them orders and they obeyed him without any delay; Kaila took off in a jog towards the house, while Kailo ran off with the flashlight in the woods behind them. Gingerly, Teleo held Lucina's head, muttering to himself in rapid Spanish.

Her body shook terribly. She could only see the outline of Teleo's face since it was so dark around them. Her whole body was numb, burning, as though something hot were crawling underneath her skin.

"Calm yourself, Luci," Teleo said softly. "Now you need to relax, to breathe in and out, in and out, that's it. You need to just close your eyes and relax."

Soon, Kailo came back and he leaned over to say to Teleo in Spanish that he had seen the snake.

"It is a *micrurus fulvius:* The red and yellow rings are touching. We need to get her some red elm and alcatan immediately, and strap her leg," Kailo said in fast Spanish.

Nodding, Teleo quickly ordered Kailo to help him carry Lucina to the house. Lucina felt faint and nearly hysterical with fear, and tears fell haphazardly on her face. His arm came up underneath her, and together with Kailo, they carried their frightened patient quickly up the stairs of the front porch, into the living room, then into a red bedroom.

They laid Lucina down on a comfortable bed, and told her to continue the breathing exercises. Some minutes later, Kailo came in with a bowl and mortar, explaining that they would be applying a special herbal cure to the bite, and that although it might hurt somewhat, it was necessary. Lucina looked at Teleo as he started his task, noticing how firmly and quietly he attended to her ankle. After a minute or so, the fire seemed to lessen and she chanced to peek at her leg; her ankle looked swollen, yet she couldn't see anything else.

When Kailo left the room, Teleo placed a piece of wood alongside Lucina's lower left leg, explaining that he was doing this to immobilize the leg as much as possible so that the healing would be more rapid. Then, he delicately started wrapping her leg and the piece of wood with a white cloth, leaving the ankle half exposed.

"Luci, you've been bitten by a snake, a pretty dangerous snake. It is called around here the fire snake, because when it bites, you feel a fire. The coral snake is rare, it hides in the woods around these parts, but don't worry: I have dealt with this snake once before so I know what I'm doing. This bite is neurotoxic, meaning it affects your respiratory system among other things. What's important is to breathe calmly like I taught you and to just stay relaxed. You might bleed from the nose, feel some pain in the ankle, and if you feel numbness, weakness or anything else, I want you to tell us. You're in good hands, Lucina, Kailo and I will take good care of you," he said, while he began applying the herbal medicine to her ankle.

After his procedure, he handed Lucina a bitter tea and when she finished drinking it, she began to feel very drowsy and soon fell asleep. The last thing she heard him say was, "*Buenas noches, flora*" and then, darkness caved in on her.

Chapter 5

When Lucina opened her eyes, it was day and although the room was well shaded from the hot rays of the sun, it was much warmer in the little red room than previously. Teleo was sitting by the window when she awoke, his eyes closed, his shoulders slouched, and his mouth slightly opened. He quickly turned to look at his patient with a worried look. His beige shirt was stained with some greenish mixture, his hair dishevelled, and bags were apparent under his brilliant eyes.

Lucina could tell he hadn't slept much. She asked him if she could remove the bed sheets, but he seemed shocked that she should mention such a thing. Teleo advised her that she had a fever, that it would be best to remain covered, and stressed that she drink a lot of water, relax, sleep a lot, and not move her leg at all.

He brought his patient a glass of water, which she drank eagerly because she was extremely thirsty. As she settled back down into the comfortable bed, Lucina thanked him for his kindness but he only nodded his head, encouraging her to go back to sleep.

*　　*　　*

It was night again when Lucina awoke, and although her sleep had been disturbing, she felt somewhat less discombobulated than before. When Teleo brought her a soup which had a lot of garlic in it, she took the bowl from his hands, thanked him, and sipped it slowly. *How terrifically good his mixture is*, she noted. *I am lucky to be in such good hands.*

"Thank you Teleo, for your kindness," she said, when she had finished the delicious soup. Teleo took the bowl from her hands and then sat down in the chair next to the bed, passing his hands through his hair with a tired look on his face.

"It's only normal, Luci, that I should take care of you," he replied, as he looked her in the eye. "After all, you are a very special woman. You've recuperated very well from the bite, much more than I expected. You must have a warrior's heart to not have lacked air."

"Lacked air?" Lucina cried out.

"Well, you see, some people react very badly to this venom and can eventually stop breathing, even if the proper remedies are given," Teleo answered softly. "I knew a boy once who was treated with such herbs but was too weak and he suffocated."

"Oh my Lord!" Lucina said with great emotion. She sank back down into the pillows and looked up at the ceiling. "You mean to say that you saved my life with your herbs?"

"No, you saved your own life."

"I don't understand!"

"You wanted to live and the herbs gave you strength to live through the night," Teleo said, as he gently tucked his patient in. Lucina felt suddenly very weak again, and as she was about to drop off to sleep again, Teleo murmured, "Lucina, you have more to do in this world before you die, I am certain of that."

She felt someone push her hair out of her face, and then, darkness hit again.

*   *   *

Lucina felt better the next day. The pain in her left leg was much less present, the dizziness and numbness had altogether disappeared, and she felt less edgy. Noticing that Teleo was not around and wondering about the delicious smell hanging in the air, she ventured out of the bed she had been lying in for more than a day and a half. Careful not to put weight on her left leg, she opened the door and peeked out into the living room. Bright sunlight blinded her as she limped slowly towards the kitchen. When she walked into the brightly lit kitchen, Teleo looked up. He was stirring some food on the stove and had been staring out the window.

"Oh, Luci, you're out of bed. Maybe you should stay there, I'm just cooking something for you and will bring it to you in a moment," he said with a tired smile.

"Thank you, Teleo. I think I need to get up a bit, even though my ankle is still hurting me," she answered, as she sat down at the table.

Lucina passed her hands through her hair and then became conscious that she must look like hell after almost two days spent in bed with a high fever. Quietly, she snuck out of the kitchen and entered the bathroom. A pale face looked back at her in the mirror. It was then that she noticed her clothes.

"I wasn't wearing this the last time I remember," she muttered out loud, staring at her white cotton pants and blue t-shirt. The thought hit her that someone had changed her clothes and put her into some new ones. Swallowing with difficulty, Lucina smoothed out her t-shirt and wandered back into the kitchen.

Well, he will have seen it all then, she thought, trying to repress her mounting embarrassment. *And there isn't much to see anyhow.*

Teleo brought her a burrito with a salad on the side of the plate. She again noticed the dark circles under his eyes as well as the big stain on his t-shirt. He smiled and plopped himself down in front of her, indicating to her that she should eat.

Slowly, Lucina bit into the burrito. An explosion of red peppers, garlic, onions, beans, and rice greeted her. She nodded her head in appreciation.

This man has saved my life, she reflected, staring intensely at Teleo as he began eating. *This Mexican, with his herbs, has pulled me out of the snake's venom and set me back on my own two feet. How can I ever thank him for all that he has done for me these past two days?*

Lucina fidgeted nervously in her chair, swallowed carefully another bite, and then began to speak.

"Teleo, I really am grateful for all that you have done, and I wish that I could thank you in some way," she said, setting down her fork and knife gently. *Oh, that sounds terrible*, she thought. *What the hell am I saying? Has the snake affected my speech too?*

"I already told you, Lucina, that you saved yourself. I was only there as support. But in fact, there is something you can do to thank me. You can take a short walk with me after lunch, outside, I think fresh air will indeed do you some good, but first, let's remove your brace. You don't need it anymore."

He pushed his empty plate aside, moved to Lucina's side and without looking at her, kneeled down on the floor and lifted her jogging pants slowly up to her knees. Lucina felt like running out of the kitchen then, but instead, she looked out the kitchen window, trying to think of something else other than his hands on her leg. He carefully undid the wooden brace, studied the bite, nodded in satisfaction, smiled at Lucina, and then rolled down her pants.

Lucina breathed a sigh of relief.

Once the dishes done, Teleo put his shoes on and handed Lucina her running shoes. Opening the screen door for her, he made a gesture indicating that his guest should pass first. Lucina thanked him and went out unto the porch, the heat and the sun, the chirping birds, and the little Mexican families driving by in their pick-up trucks.

After sickness, everything seems so much more alive and promising. The little house which first had seemed a yellow, unfriendly shack now seemed charming, cozy and welcoming. The palm trees which at first had seemed dry and mundane now carried a vibrant energy as they wavered in the afternoon heat. The tall grass around the property seemed softer, more inviting.

Teleo offered his left arm and still somewhat shaky, Lucina accepted it. It was the first time she was actually close to him, at least in her normal state of mind. Her stomach clenched and her heart skipped a beat. *Pull yourself together*, she angrily thought. *I won't be a little ditz.*

They walked in silence on the narrow dirt road. Lucina noticed how lovely Señora Labotta's neighborhood was. A few houses were scattered along the dirt road, palm trees and other tropical trees bordered the peaceful road, and the whole scenery looked like a pre-civilization scene. The noon sun was hot, the air somewhat humid, and the clouds offered some moments of coolness. Lucina felt rejuvenated.

"How's your left leg?" Teleo said, looking down at her.

"I still feel some pain sometimes, but right now, it's all right. At least the numbness has gone away," she replied, glancing down at her leg hidden in her white pants.

They continued to walk slowly. *How strong he is*, Lucina mused. She quickly glanced at his shoulders and noticed how square they were, even through his thick, green t-shirt. As his hair gently wavered in the wind, Teleo turned and looked at Lucina intensely, his mouth parting slightly.

"Lucina, is there something wrong?"

She stopped walking in sudden fright and tried to avert his look, yet there was something magnetic about his eyes, and she found herself incapable of looking elsewhere. She began to feel dizzy again, closed her eyes and responded that she was feeling still a little nauseous but that it was nothing to worry about. Nodding his head in genuine sympathy, Teleo turned back towards the house while Lucina chewed nervously on her lip.

What she really wanted to tell him was that there was nothing wrong. Ever since she had met him and his mother, her life had started to have meaning again. She still wasn't sure in what way, but there was a seed that had been planted and it was beginning to grow slowly. She wanted to let him know how beautiful his eyes were, how gracious his movements were, but of course Lucina lacked the courage to say all these things. She preferred to talk about the sights of nature than her own feelings; she had never been good at expressing her true feelings to anyone.

Although Lucina and Teleo didn't walk very far, the time outside in the sunlight did help her clear her mind. She was truly content as they made their way back to the pretty little house. Teleo opened the door for her again and Lucina felt another wave of heat going through her body. Trying not to let her emotions show, she walked past him into the cool living room.

"What's with the eagles?" she asked Teleo, as she stared at the tapestry.

"Oh, the eagles. Well, some say that eagles are more evolved than humans. They pick one mate and stay with their mate throughout their entire lives, even if the mate dies. Some say that eagles have understood true love."

*   *   *

That evening, Kailo and Kaila came over once more, and all four of them ate on the porch outside while Señora Labotta's sleepy golden eyes stared up at them occasionally. Lucina paid more attention to the words being exchanged in Spanish and at one moment, thought she heard Kailo congratulating Teleo on his fine medicine work.

Lucina looked down at her leg and shuddered.

After supper, she asked Teleo if she could use the phone to call her mother. Teleo replied that she didn't have to ask anymore. She excused herself, went to the living room phone and dialed her mother's number.

"Hi mom," she said as her mother's voice came through on the other end. "How are you?"

"*Figlia*, you could have called earlier," was the stern reply. "You call Stacey before you call me. How's Mexico?"

Lucina hesitated. She didn't want to tell her mother about the meeting with Señora Labotta and Teleo, it would upset her and worry her to death probably. Her mother had always been paranoid, anxious and deeply religious. Anything that was out of the ordinary, such as camping on the land of strange Mexicans, was incomprehensible to her. It was normal though. Her mother was a war child, had grown up at the end of the Second World War in Italy and had terrible scars. For instance, she could never throw anything away; her house was a huge garbage can of thousands of little useless objects. Lucina knew that it wasn't her mother's fault that she was so paranoid, but sometimes, it got to her.

It is best not to mention anything strange, Lucina concluded. She told her mother that her trip was going fine, that Mexicans were very nice people, and that the food was much better than the food in Montreal. She also related how she wasn't eating meat at all and feeling good about it. Lucina's mother was very happy to hear all this, and probed her about how she was feeling, mentally.

"Oh, mom, you know, there are good days, and there are bad days," Lucina said. *I won't tell her about being bitten by a snake, that would make her have a heart attack,* Lucina reasoned. "It's been wonderful so far, I think Doctor Field was right in sending me here."

Lucina's mother asked her a few more questions, and relieved that her daughter was alive and well, finally hung up the phone. *I have done a good deed,* Lucina congratulated herself. *I have caused less anxiety in the world today by lying. Sometimes not telling the truth can save people heart attacks.*

"Señorita, *que estás haciendo allí?*" Kailo called out from the porch.

Lucina stood up and called to him that she would be out in a minute. She went to the bathroom, closed and locked the door. Leaning against the door, she stared straight in front of her, out the dusty little rectangular window.

So much has happened over the past few days, she reflected. *How in the world did tiny little herbs cure me? Back home, I would probably have waited hours at the hospital, on the verge of death. Maybe I would never have received an antidote since there would have been no competent doctors around, because of government cut-backs in the health system. And then even if I had received an antidote, it would have probably been expired, again because of cut-backs in the health system. I would have been surrounded by little Hispanic nurses repeating to each other that I looked terrible, but who knew what I had really? The nurse taking care of me would have certainly been grumpy, sleepy and annoyed because she would have just worked another fifteen hour shift, of course, due to cut-backs.*

"God, what a strange holiday this has turned into," Lucina sighed, as a firefly outside the window snapped her out of her wandering thoughts.

"Lucina, are you feeling okay?" Teleo's voice rang out from behind the bathroom door. She quickly responded that she was all right, just feeling a little nauseous again. As Teleo walked away, Lucina straightened up and stared at her reflection in the mirror.

"Okay, Luci, you can do it. You can be happy again. You can do it."

A little Dr. Phil once in a while never killed anyone.

On the porch, Kailo and Kaila were slowly rocking in their rocking chairs, while Teleo sat on the loveseat not far from them, flipping pages of a herbal magazine. He looked up at Lucina when she walked out of the house, smiling warmly at her. She sat herself in the lawn chair near the group and started to join in on the discussion. Teleo was explaining how America had lost its path in the world of pharmaceuticals.

"They want to make money, so they brainwash people into thinking that pills will solve all their problems," he was saying, pointing to a picture in his magazine. It was a photo of two older people smiling, with the ocean in the background. *It is a lovely picture*, Lucina thought. "They'll probably make it illegal to cure people with herbs soon. For thousands of years, humans have survived due to herbs, but now the big businesses want to make profit and they know people will swallow anything they give them. I'm glad that in Mexico at least we still know the value of real medicine."

Kailo lifted his hands up to the skies and nodded his head dramatically.

"Herbs are God's gift to humans," Teleo continued. "People have lost their faith, if you ask me. When you cease believing in the power of nature, you have lost your way."

Lucina pondered this for a while. How true it sounded to her ears. When Teleo looked at her and asked her what she thought of the pharmaceutical industry, Lucina fidgeted in her seat slightly, searching for her words.

"Well, I think that antibiotics have helped humans live much longer, and that they will keep improving our life. I also think, though, now that I have been cured by herbs that maybe we should also incorporate natural medicine into our lives again."

Kailo and Kaila didn't answer and continued rocking in the rocking chairs. Lucina began to feel as though Teleo and she were the only ones present on the porch. He put his arms behind his head and closed his eyes, looking like he was in deep reflection.

A few minutes later, Kailo and Kaila got up and declared that they would be going home. Kailo emphasized how happy they were that Lucina was doing better and mentioned that perhaps they all might have a chance to see one another again before Lucina left for Canada the following week. The foursome shook hands and then Teleo and Lucina watched the couple get into their car.

Sighing, Teleo leaned against the banister and observed his friends disappear into the night. He was wearing a long-sleeved faded blue shirt with the words *Sea Feliz* sprawled in yellow across his chest. Although Lucina thought it was a cheesy slogan, she didn't want to offend him by making fun of it. A sudden nervousness invaded her stomach, and she stared at the ground in front of her. *There it is again,* Lucina reflected. *This feeling. Whenever Teleo is around, I feel this fire coming through me.*

"Luci, are you tired? Perhaps you should sleep now, to recuperate your energy," Teleo said softly. "Tomorrow we could maybe go see a beautiful cave nearby, if you're feeling better."

She looked into his radiant eyes, feeling as though something inside of her were melting. *God, how a man can be so beautiful!* she wondered silently. *Men are beautiful for a short while until they want to spread your legs and spread their masculinity everywhere, until they dump you for the next pretty blond, or until they get tired of you and decide to seek other adventures. Men tire so easily of women.*

Lucina agreed with him and wished him a good night. They smiled at each other, then Lucina turned on her heel to head for the bathroom. *It's no use sticking around,* she concluded. *If I do, it will only lead to trouble, and that's the last thing I need right now, more trouble.*

Teleo brewed a tea for Lucina while she was in the bathroom. It was Cramp bark and Rosemary to help her muscles relax and to aid in blood circulation. She drank it alone in her new room as she lay on the soft mattress. *I am glad I don't have to sleep in my tent,* she thought happily. *At least there's one good thing about having a near-death experience: People always treat you better after you nearly die.*

Chapter 6

When she opened her eyes the next morning, Lucina felt rejuvenated and almost back to her usual self. She drew the sheets back, looked at her left ankle, and with joy noted that the inflammation had almost vanished. With lightness in her heart, she put on blue jeans, a faded black t-shirt and combed her hair quickly before going into the kitchen. To her surprise Señora Labotta was sitting on the couch drinking a tea. Her bright brown eyes stared intensely at her and a familiar wave of nervousness moved in Lucina.

"I heard about the coral snake," she said slowly, looking at Lucina's leg. "How is your leg? Did Teleo take good care of you?"

"Yes, he did, thank you. My leg is better, and I feel much better today. How is your father?" Lucina replied, moving closer to the couch.

"He will survive. Nothing serious. But do sit down for a bit, señorita, I have something to speak to you about," the Mexican said in an abrupt tone.

Lucina felt the color rising to her face and felt like three years old, about to be reprimanded for having done something bad. She sat herself down immediately and clasped her hands together while Señora Labotta looked at Lucina and nodded her head, as if confirming something.

"You know, ever since you arrived here, I have been think-

ing about your spirit. Why do you think you were bitten by a
snake the other night?"

Lucina's mouth dropped opened and she stared at Señora
Labotta for a few seconds. Finally, she answered that she had
no idea why she had been bitten and that she had no clue what
her spirit and the snakebite had to do with one another. Señora Labotta put her tea down, sighed, and then explained to
Lucina that all sickness was a direct message from the spirit to
the body. Lucina's snakebite, then, had a very strong message
attached to it, and her job was to decipher it.

"What do you think it means, this snake bite?" Lucina
questioned Señora Labotta, curious.

Señora Labotta was quiet for a few seconds, her eyes
closed.

"The snake within you has awakened," she finally replied.

"The snake in me?"

"The snake in you. The energy which propagates all life,
the one in the Bible which is referred to as 'Satan'. You see,
people have completely misunderstood that symbol, I am certain that Teleo has told you about that already, it is his favorite
subject. The snake in the garden of Eve was not Satan: It was
the all-powerful sexual energy within us humans. The snake
is the tree of knowledge. That knowledge is that all humans
have in them a divine essence, and this divine essence is their
sexuality. It was woman who first came into contact with her
sexual divine energy and who then led man to his real source.
With this in mind, Eve no longer becomes the terrible sinner:
She becomes the first one to discover her true godly nature.
When Eve encountered the serpent, she encountered her own
divine sexual energy, and that energy is the most powerful energy there is. It is God's energy, or whatever you choose to call
God. That is why Eve and Adam were thrown out of Eden,
because they came into contact with their true divine selves,

and the Christian God does not deal well with competition."

Señora Labotta took a sip of her tea, pausing to let Lucina digest these words.

"Of course, in all religions or nearly all religions, sexuality is synonymous with sin. Do you see why people cannot even begin to understand the power of their own sexuality? Because for so long sexuality has been seen as evil, as something bad, wrong, disgusting. The notion of Evil or Satan exists only because Satan is easier to deal with than one's divine sexual nature. Once people stop fearing, they will see a whole new garden in front of them, one filled with divine sexuality instead of this Satan figure."

Lucina was shocked by these words and remained silent for a few seconds, digesting what had just been said. *If my mother were around*, she thought, *she would faint. This is too much for her poor, harvested mind.*

"That is really something," Lucina replied. "So this snake-bite has something to do with my sexual awakening?"

"That is my interpretation, señorita. Now you give it a try."

"Well, if I am sexually awakening as you say, I hope I won't get kicked out of Eden because my mother would be terribly upset about it," Lucina answered.

Señora Labotta laughed uproariously, patting her guest's knee. Lucina was surprised at the outburst because Señora Labotta had never laughed like that before then.

"There is no Eden, my dear child. It is part of the Christian creation. What there is, is a world devoid of any true, magical sexual energy. I do not mean lust. I mean the true, magical heat which is found in the stomach, and which is responsible for all living things. When you begin to feel this heat, let me know. Then you will have stepped out of the past constructed world, Eden, and into the new world, your own Self. Remember when I said to you all roads cross at you? That is what it means. You are the center of your world and you must become aware of it. After that, what you choose to do with your energy is your business."

Lucina sat as though she had been electrocuted. Señora Labotta got up, leaving her guest sitting like a dumb statue.

Lord, I am happy my mother will never meet this woman, Lucina was thinking.

*   *   *

"Today, I will take you to my special place," Teleo said with a smile a few hours later.

Curious, Lucina asked him where this "special place" was but Teleo refused to give her any hint. Instead, he told her to go prepare herself for some horse-back riding. Excitedly, Lucina took a cold shower, put on some new clothes, and packed some food in a bag pack. She remembered that she had to do some weeding that day to catch up on the days she hadn't done anything.

After having wished Señora Labotta a nice day and thanking her for the use of her room during her cure, Lucina went to the stable and peered in. Luna looked up at her and whinnied. Teleo carried two heavy duffle bags into the barn and placed them across the back of his horse, while Lucina stared curiously at the bags, wondering what was inside them.

They rode for some time, passing near the rapids, through several fields, and near a few, colorful Mexican houses. As the sun beat down upon their sweating backs, Lucina started to hope that they would come to a rest because she felt tired all of a sudden.

Teleo pointed to a sloping hill and told Lucina that they were almost at the cave. They urged their strong horses up the steep hill, and then at last came upon a secluded area. The cave was enclosed in high rocks and moss grew on the rocks, reminding Lucina of a scene from the movie *The Lord of the Rings*. The opening of the cave was not more than eight feet high by four feet wide, and as she was looking at the opening, Lucina was hit by a wave of anxiety. *What does he want with me here in this cave?* Lucina thought in a panic. *What are his intentions?*

"Here we are," Teleo exclaimed. They got down from their horses and tied them to a large pine tree. Teleo swung the two bags over his shoulder, telling Lucina to follow him. When she saw him nearing the mouth of the cave, her fears came screaming up in her, and she became uneasy once again. Teleo turned to look at his companion.

"It's all right, you can trust me, Lucina. I won't hurt you," he said in a soft voice. Lucina smiled uncertainly, looked around her, and noticed that there was dead silence. No bird chirped, no wind blew, no human spoke. She was really alone with him now.

She followed Teleo rather reluctantly into the narrow cave. Once inside, she noticed how cool the temperature was and started to feel calmer when she noticed that it was not quite as dark inside as she had first imagined. The cave was only about twenty feet long and ten feet across, and water flowed out of a pair of gigantic boulders at the back of the cave, creating a serene, relaxing sound.

"A perfect place to meditate," Teleo said, as he pulled out two colorful blankets from the bags. He also lit incense and a strong odor began to fill the cave. He sat himself down, cross-legged, and invited Lucina to join him.

"Luci, this is where I wanted to take you," he said softly, as she settled herself down in front of him. "They say this place has powerful healing energies. Shamans used to frequent this cave hundreds of years ago. It is believed that in such caves, shamans connected themselves to the sacred energy of the earth and sometimes they would bring crystals to channel the earth's energy. What is really interesting is that in some caves in Mexico, the Mayan shamans used to practice blood letting and even sacrificed victims. In caves with deep wells of water, Mayan kings threw virgins in to appease the gods. These places, *cenotes,* can be found at various locations across Mexico. For example, Chichen Itza has a famous *cenote* in which many human bones and pottery have been found."

Lucina looked up at the ceiling of the cave and noticed how smooth the rock was.

"Anyone sacrificed here?" she asked, with a shaky grin. She was having trouble breathing: Her anxiety had returned.

"Not a chance," Teleo laughed. "The Zapotecs and Mixtecs around here didn't practice human sacrifice. Kailo used to bring me out here whenever he felt I needed the earth's healing energies, so I thought that maybe you might benefit from this cave too."

Lucina nodded, feeling the familiar wave of nervousness move through her body. *Oh God, why have I come here?* she thought. *I don't want to start anything I can't finish. Should I tell him about what happened with the last man? How I ran away like a chicken when the first signs of love appeared?*

"If you like," Teleo said, interrupting Lucina's negative thoughts. "I can give you a massage, it is another of my specialties as a healer."

Lucina looked up at him, panicked. *This is what it's all about!* she thought angrily. *He pretends he's all spiritual and then he takes me to this cave and wants to "massage me"? Men are all the same, they only want one thing: Booty.*

Teleo's eyes found hers and she magically relaxed under his gaze. *Stop thinking so negatively,* she reprimanded herself.

"Teleo, I don't know. I don't really like massages," Lucina answered, fumbling for a good excuse. In reality, she wanted his hands to touch her again like they had the other day on her leg.

"I'm offering you a free healing session, if you're interested, but I won't be offended if you refuse," he replied. Something in his eyes told her otherwise.

Doctor Field's words came rushing back to her then. One session prior to Lucina's departure to Mexico had been on the subject of opening up to men, and accepting that men had different ways of expressing love than women did.

"Lucina," Doctor Field had patiently explained, "Men are different from women. They need physical proof of love, whereas women need more verbal proof. Even if you deny it, I know this to be a fact. Just because men like sex doesn't make them pigs, it makes them human, it makes them the other half. Men like to feel the truth in their bodies, women in their minds. It does not make one sex better than the other."

Lucina had frowned, crumpling up some Kleenex.

"Right, Doctor Field. Men are just so easy to get. Their brains are configured for one thing, and one thing only: Sexual intercourse. I have never met a man who was different. It doesn't exist."

Doctor Field had laughed and scribbled something down in his notes.

Teleo's soft eyes brought Lucina back into the present. She stared down at the earth and took some cold earth in her hands, letting it pass through her shaky fingers. *I know my limits and I will set them,* she told herself with confidence.

"Okay, mister Mexican herbal healer, but no funny business. I used to do kung fu and I wouldn't want to hurt you," she finally replied, giving him a serious look.

Teleo held up his hands, swearing an oath to the cave gods that he would respect Lucina. She laughed at his exaggerated gesture. Carefully, she laid down on her stomach on

the soft, colorful blanket, trying to act indifferent and care-
free, as though she had been massaged hundreds of times in a
Mexican cave by a firm, muscular, emerald-eyed herbalist and
historian.

Lucina stiffened involuntarily at his touch and tried to
think of random things, such as what Stacey might be doing at that moment or what her mother might be cooking.
She pictured her small but comfortable apartment and hoped
her mother was taking care of dusting, especially along the
window because dust collected faster there than other places.
She thought of how it was probably snowing in Montreal, and
how the streets would be slushy and dirty.

Lucina's thoughts vanished as Teleo started gently massaging her calves, first using his palm, then his fingers. She
closed her eyes, turned her head away from Teleo's and focused on her breathing. Her heart started pounding away like
a hammer in her chest.

"You can relax, I won't hurt you," Teleo said softly. "I feel
that your body contains many memories of anger, pain, and
loneliness."

How does he know that? she pondered.

"Anger is a terrible enemy of the body, it can really eat you
up inside if you don't find a way to let it out completely."

Lucina felt his warm hands upon her body and realized
she had never been touched so powerfully before. He seemed
to know where her muscles were aching, where the pain was
lodged. Slowly, all thoughts disappeared, her heart continued
to pound like a hammer, and all she could feel was Teleo's
strong hands tracing an invisible map on her tired body, trying
to understand her pain, her suffering, her scars. A sudden heat
formed in her stomach.

"Many have forgotten the body," Teleo murmured. "They
focus too much on the mind. Philosophy is outdated. We must

live the truth in our bodies, not in our minds. The only way to reach truth is by physically living through illusion. Your healing can only be found through your body's healing."

Lucina heard his words, as if they were a river flowing through her veins. Slowly, she felt her body melting under his touch, as though she were becoming pure air. It was a sensation she had never felt before in her life.

"But to live in the body does not mean to live for pleasure, as some have wrongly asserted," continued Teleo in his soft, hypnotic voice. "It simply means to re-claim the body in which our soul has planted itself. It means to feel reality, not only see it. It means to touch reality, and then pierce the lies. The real masters learned to transcend illusion with their bodies. Jesus and many other prophets ascended to the Other World with their bodies, and they knew the importance of the body. In reality, the Bible revealed only part of the truth; the real truth is that all humans, once connected fully to their bodies, can evolve with their bodies and carry their bodies to the Other World. I like to call this the Resurrection Phase. One day soon, people will transcend death, old age, and leave this world with their bodies, as Jesus once did. When they grasp their body's power, they shall grasp the power of the snake and then they shall reach total freedom."

Lucina was only half listening to Teleo's hypnotic words. Heat, waves of heat invaded her entire body and she felt as though she were burning from the inside out. Leaning over, Teleo whispered in her ear that she should erase all fears, all thoughts and let the fire burn her. Lucina didn't understand what was happening, but neither did she care to. She simply wanted to feel, for what seemed like the first time in her life, her body, her limbs, her heart. Her head began to throb intensely.

Teleo's massage lasted for what seemed eternity. Finally, he sat down not far from Lucina and observed her in the semi-darkness. His hair cascaded like a dark waterfall across his face, and as he brushed his hair back, Lucina glimpsed his soft, brown skin glowing in the semi-darkness.

"You survived the fire," he said to her with a smile.

"The fire?" she said, somewhat groggily.

"Yes, the fire. This place is where Kailo brought me to purify me before I became a healer and I wanted to give you what he gave me years ago."

"Oh," she answered, unable to make any sense of his words.

"I will leave you alone, now, and go outside for a bit. When you feel strong, just come and get me," he said softly, leaving Lucina on her stomach feeling like she had just experienced the first real physical contact with her inner being.

This is what sex should feel like, she concluded.

*   *   *

Some minutes later, Lucina reluctantly got up and went looking for Teleo. He was outside near the stream, staring absentmindedly at the rushing water. She walked over to where he was sitting and lightly touched his shoulder.

"Thanks, for whatever you did back there. I feel a hundred times lighter," she said gently, at last understanding that this man was a rare specimen of the male species: He had kept his word.

He smiled, standing up.

"The pleasure was all mine, shall we go back now?"

Lucina smiled back.

Chapter 7

The following day, Teleo was not there to eat breakfast with Lucina. He had had errands to run and was going to be absent most of the day. Pretending that it didn't bother her in the least, she put on her jeans, a pale pink baby tee and walked up to the house. When she entered the yellow house, Señora Labotta was already eating at the small table. She looked up and indicated that her guest should sit down. The omelette looked delicious.

That morning, Señora Labotta asked Lucina what she thought of love. Lucina felt rather uneasy when the Mexican brought the subject up, but remembering that nothing had happened with Teleo, and that nothing would anyway, Lucina soon relaxed under her host's gaze.

"What is love?" Señora Labotta repeated, taking a sip of her green tea.

"Oh, I don't know what love is," Lucina replied, sighing. *If I knew, I wouldn't have suffered so much in the past*, she wanted to add.

"Love has many facets, señorita, many facets. You see, the beginning is so easy, so much fun, so many things to discover, so many things to say...it's like a big fiesta if you will. It is easy to lose oneself in love, in the other. However, the test is to stay yourself no matter what, to grow side by side with the other, but never obscure yourself or the other. If you will, it is like the number II."

"This number," Señora Labotta explained as she traced the roman number on the table with her finger, "Is the best way to explain true love between humans. You see two lines standing straight one next to the other. Yet notice how the lines are connected to the ground and to the heavens. In other words, the lines are connected to the sky and the earth, to the physical and the spiritual. There are always two lines, always two people, two entities. If this rule is forgotten, love is forgotten. One loses oneself in the other, and then love no longer exists. What exists is addiction, fatigue, dependence, and eventually, jealousy, hatred, envy and maybe even death. Many women have the tendency to attach themselves and lose their own person in love, more than men."

"The real test, señorita," the Mexican woman continued as she took another bite of her omelette, "Is knowing how to flow in love and how to hold unto oneself during the whole process. This is not an easy thing, señorita, not an easy thing."

Studying her host's face, Lucina asked Señora Labotta whether she had ever been in love. Señora Labotta answered that she had been, with Teleo's father. They met, she explained, one sunny afternoon in a garden. She had been looking at the flowers around her when all of a sudden, their eyes had met. There was no doubt for her, she said. Roberto was her soul mate, or at least one of her soul mates; she could feel him from dozens of feet away. Lucina questioned her about their life together. The Mexican told her that they had started the bookstore together, had travelled to Europe every year to explore new countries, and had had Teleo four years after their marriage. Lucina was afraid to ask what had happened to Roberto, but Señora Labotta answered her question in a few words.

"He died, one day, unexpectedly, while I was working in my bookstore," she replied, turning her head to look out the kitchen window. "After Roberto, it took many years before I felt like I could love again. No other soul mate presented itself, so I remained alone. I rather be alone than with someone who will not help me evolve."

"I'm sorry to hear that," Lucina murmured gently, not knowing what else to say.

"Yes, death is a very big test for true love, a very big test,"
Señora Labotta said. "I still feel his spirit around me even though
his body is gone. When I am alone at night, I feel that he is standing next to me, watching me, whispering things in my ear that
only I can understand. When I walk with clients at the bookstore,
he is with me, watching me, guiding me. But señorita, you should
not worry about death now, you should worry about life. You are
young and have so much to live for."

Lucina looked up at her and for the first time since she had
met Señora Labotta, she felt hope. Señora Labotta nodded her
head, patted Lucina's small hand and encouraged her to eat.

*   *   *

The afternoon was long. Lucina weeded many hours, just because
she wanted to get rid of Teleo's face, his eyes, his hands, his words.
Most of all his touch; it had affected her profoundly and she
wanted to keep her mind busy. She tried to avoid any further talk
with Señora Labotta about things related to love that day.

In the late afternoon, she took the bus and went to the market in the city to browse around. There she bought a little Virgin
Mary statue made out of pottery for her mother, even though her
mother already had a dozen at home. Lucina knew that one from
Mexico would please her immensely. For herself, she bought a
long red sleeveless dress with white flowers along the bottom
and the neck line, and bought some guava and kiwi which she
thought Señora Labotta might appreciate.

When Lucina got back to the house, Teleo had returned and
was in the kitchen, helping his mother cut vegetables. He gave
Lucina a quick smile when he saw her walk in, indicating that
she should have a seat. He was wearing torn jeans, a tight fitting

green t-shirt and his hair was tied back with an elastic. Lucina glanced at his hands and flashes of the previous day entered her mind.

"So, you have been quite the professional weeder today!" he commented to Lucina, as he handed her some chips and salsa. Lucina shrugged, grinning. She was happy that he had noticed her work. Maybe he was actually impressed by something she had done.

"Miss Canada has been learning quite a few things today," piped in Señora Labotta. She continued cutting carrots effortlessly and tossing them into a huge pot on the stove.

"Yes, indeed," Lucina replied, eating her chips with new energy.

Chapter 8

Lucina's last week with the Labotta's was entertaining and unforgettable. She spent many evenings walking with Teleo on the main road, talking about life, the past, friendships, even relationships. She grew to love his company, his presence, his intensity, his voice. Little by little, she opened up to him, and told him little bits about her life in Montreal that she rarely told anyone. She revealed her feeling of loneliness and isolation, and admitted to him that she didn't like programming computers that much and that she had chosen that domain because it came with a good salary. She also explained how her relationship with her mother was strained and stressful, something she rarely told anyone. Teleo was an attentive listener and gave her good advice.

They soon became inseparable, spending every minute together. Teleo brought his guest to many different spots in the jungle, pointing out the different plants as they went along, teaching her about how Mexicans used certain roots to cure even cancers. Lucina was skeptical about this but Teleo assured her that herbs were quite powerful in curing cancers.

"For instance," he told her, "Did you know that yarrow is good against lung cancer? And if you use it daily, it prevents lung cancer. But of course, people prefer radiation to herbs."

Lucina had asked him more about herbs. She was curious because she had never learned about such things before.

"What do you take, say when you have a cold?" she questioned him.

"Many plants are good against the common cold. You can take echinacea root to boost your immune system, ginger for a sore throat and upset stomach, yarrow against infection. Euca lyptus is good against congestion and coughs, as well as linden and elder. But one of the most common herbs you can find on the market that is super powerful is garlic. Garlic is known to increase the libido, is good against all types of infections, reduces cholesterol, and helps one have a better blood circulation. The list is endless."

Lucina was impressed by Teleo's herbal knowledge and even imagined for a few seconds she could learn his trade. Maybe she could change her profession and become a naturopath instead of a computer programmer. She laughed inwardly: She couldn't picture herself studying herbs all day, she would go nuts and besides, didn't learning herbs entail learning Latin?

She continued to help Señora Labotta with the weeding as well as the cooking. Teleo taught her how to make burritos, enchiladas, and even tortillas. Lucina enjoyed learning because at home she never had taken the time to cook. Señora Labotta was around mostly at night and during that time, the threesome played cards occasionally. Lucina taught her new friends Crazy Eights, as well as her favorite game of all time, *Trou du cul.* Teleo had a good laugh when he found out what the name of the game really meant.

The morning before her last day in Mexico, Lucina awoke feeling nervous and light-headed. She didn't comprehend why she was feeling so strange, but she knew that horse-back riding might clear her head a little, as it always had in the past.

"*Buenos días,*" she said as Señora Labotta walked up to her.

"So, it is your last day, señorita. What will you do today?" Señora Labotta asked Lucina, carefully observing her.

"Oh, I have no idea," Lucina answered, looking at a colorful bird perched not far from them. "I was thinking maybe of doing a little horse-back riding, you know, just for old time's sake."

Señora Labotta nodded in agreement and told Lucina that she was most welcome to take Luna out for a ride. Lucina thanked her, and looking around for Teleo, she spotted him near the back of the house, clearing some bushes. He was shirtless that day. Lucina noticed his beautifully carved back glittering in the early morning sun.

"Hello Teleo," she said, as she walked up to him. He looked up, grinned, and wiped the sweat from his face.

"*Hola*, Luci! *Como estás hoy?*"

"*Muy bien, gracias*. I thought of maybe going riding in the jungle, would you like to come with me?" she asked, watching him as he pulled out a thick branch from a pile of dead trees.

Teleo nodded, promising Lucina that he would be ready in five minutes. He dropped his ax, went into the house, cleaned himself up, and then returned with a light bag containing water bottles and some vegetables. As usual, he hadn't brought any meat but Lucina was getting used to eating vegetables instead; she felt lighter without meat in her stomach.

Settling comfortably into their saddles, Teleo and Lucina rode in silence for a while. She wanted to thank him for all the things his mother and him had done for her, but no words came out. *This always happens to me*, she thought sadly. *Whenever I am on the brink of showing gratitude, words fail me. Why oh why do words fail me when I need them the most?*

Doctor Field had told her about her blockage with words. He had also told her not to worry so much about what other people thought.

"In life, if we spend too much time formulating words, words lose their meaning. You have to pop them out like popcorn, pop pop pop. Words need to flow!" he had said one afternoon. "You can't live your life in silence. A human being is made to express herself you know, and words allow for energy to circulate. Try blurting out random thoughts sometimes, you'll see you're pretty smart."

At that moment, Lucina wanted to blurt out her thoughts but was scared she was going to blurt out a cheesy love declaration that would cause Teleo to run away. She preferred to hold her tongue, despite what she had learned back home. *Silence is my comfort,* she mused. *In it I am happy and alone.*

When they reached a clearing, Teleo suggested they stop and take a rest in the shade.

"What a nice spot," Lucina declared, looking around. They were standing on a quiet, flat land. Birds could be heard in the distance, and the only other sound was the swishing of the tall grasses that surrounded them. Teleo and Lucina sat down in the grass, looking up peacefully at the cloudless sky.

"What a lovely sky," Lucina commented, not sure of what to say. Teleo smiled. He sat with his legs in Indian style, his favorite position.

"So, what will you do back home?" he said after a few minutes, turning to look at Lucina. His green eyes bore into her soul.

"Oh, I don't know yet," Lucina replied. "Maybe find another job, you know, and move on. Hopefully forget the past."

Teleo was quiet for some time, and then, turned to look more intensely at Lucina. His lips parted and he hesitated, as though searching for the right words to say something.

"You could stay here with us, you know," he murmured. "My mother could give you a job at her store, and you could become my assistant cook. I could teach you more about herbs and you could become a herb nurse if you like."

Lucina grinned and threw a piece of grass at him.

"Sure, what a life! I am certain my mother would have a heart attack," she answered, slapping his arm. Teleo laughed and punched her back lightly on the shoulder. Lucina stopped laughing and felt her throat clenching up, remembering that this was going to be one of their last moments alone. She would leave the next day to go back to her pathetic life in Montreal. Tears started

filling up in her eyes. So that Teleo could not see her, she turned
her head away.

I don't want him to think I'm in love with him or something, she
told herself.

Teleo was looking at Lucina with a strange look. He moved
closer to her without her noticing it. Lucina closed her eyes and
when she opened them, she realized Teleo's shoulder was touching hers. He reached over, took her in his arms and clasped her
to him. Instead of kissing him, like she would have wanted to,
Lucina began to cry. She felt humiliated but she couldn't control
herself anymore; the tears fell. Lucina cried that day like a child,
not holding anything back, not worried about anything anymore.
She just wanted to cry in Teleo's arms and feel loved. Teleo remained silent, holding her head against his chest, caressing her
soft hair. For the first time in a long time, Lucina felt at home in
someone's arms.

After some time, she pulled away and straightened up. *It is
no use starting something that we cannot continue,* she told herself.
*It will only end in pain and more suffering. It's best to walk away
now.* She looked at him and detached herself from his strong
arms.

"Let's go back now," she said quietly. Teleo nodded, got up
and helped her on to her horse. His hand lingered on her leg, as
if wanting to caress it, as if he wanted to hold onto her. But he
pulled back and settled into his saddle.

*   *   *

That last night, Lucina had a very strange dream. She was standing on a sidewalk in Montreal, staring at her watch, but her
watch had weird inscriptions on it and she couldn't figure out
what was written. She threw the watch away and the scenery
changed completely. Lucina found herself in a cave, with long

shadows dancing on the walls. A tall woman wearing a red cape stood facing a wall in the dark cave, and in her right hand she held a walking stick and was chanting something in a language Lucina did not understand.

Suddenly, the cave woman whirled around and stared at Lucina, her eyes like two bright white lights. Lucina's first instinct was to run, but for some reason, she was rooted to the ground firmly.

"She who was dead has risen," the cave woman sang out in a loud, thundering voice. "She who was dead has risen and shall awake the Snake God. Only the Snake knows the path to true energy, and only the Snake shall make the past turn to dust. Rise up, see your mirror and feel the heat. The earth awakens, and with this awakening ends the lies, the deceit and the endless turmoil."

Lucina felt herself winded by the strange words and had trouble breathing.

The woman was face to face with her. Her eyes were like two burning suns.

"You, you of all people should know what love is. It is not meek, timid and tame, it is wild like the fire in this cave!" the woman shouted. All of a sudden, a fire appeared around Lucina, and her skin felt like it was burning, melting into the red heat. The woman bowed and her long red cape gathered around her.

"Let yourself burn, and you shall know the path of true love. Only through our deaths can we be re-born. Enter the fire to enter the path," the woman chanted. "Enter the fire to enter the path. Enter the fire to enter the path. Enter the fire to enter the path."

Lucina awoke with a cry.

God, how I wish I could wake Señora Labotta up and ask her about this dream, she thought to herself as she shakily sat up. *It is going to have to wait until tomorrow.*

*   *   *

Early the next morning, Lucina walked into the house and found Señora Labotta preparing some *huevos a la mexicana*. She greeted Lucina with a warm smile. Her guest sat down at the tiny kitchen table, uncertain of how to begin relating her dream. Remembering the advice of her therapist, she blurted out her dream without thinking too much about her words. Señora Labotta listened attentively and then joined Lucina at the table.

"Lucina, that is a beautiful dream," the Mexican woman commented. "It has to do with the Other."

"The Other?" Lucina asked, confused.

"The Other is the real you, your spiritual self which is whole and unafraid. The Other is the one who leads us to truth, away from our endless reincarnation here on earth. Perhaps your Other was the powerful woman healer in the cave, telling you that you must no longer fear the Snake, that powerful sexual energy that is central to life and evolution. Our beliefs of the world often keep us from reaching the Other. Religious beliefs, the past, our parents, our systems of education, they are all there to bottle up the Other. I find your dream spectacular; you should really not forget it."

"I don't understand. Isn't there only one me?" Lucina asked, more confused than ever.

"Ahh, the mistake of the West, to pretend it knows all the answers. Have you read Herman Hesse? One of his books is called *Steppenwolf* and talks about the soul as having hundreds of different personalities. What the West calls 'Split Personality Syndrome' is simply the true nature of all souls. We are not cut into stone, like the West would want us to believe; our souls move continuously like water. When you realize this, you realize that your real self is simply in constant movement. The Other is this movement of fearlessness, guiding you."

Doctor Field's words came back to Lucina; "Flow and let go, Lucina, flow and let go." Lucina wondered whether Doctor Field knew about the Other, and how the Other was like water.

"That is very interesting, thank you Señora Labotta, for the insight," Lucina said, thoughtful.

*   *   *

After breakfast it was time to pack her things and get ready for the return. Although Lucina felt a lump in her throat, she forced herself to remain calm and composed. It would do no good to begin crying now. Teleo helped her take down the tent, fold her sleeping bag, and carry her bags to the front of the house. Señora Labotta walked over to where Lucina was standing, looking lost.

"I am very happy you followed your heart," Señora Labotta said to Lucina. "Instead of fearing, you decided to come here and stay with us, without knowing who we were. That is the beginning of the journey to the heart, facing your fears. If you do not face your fears, they come back to haunt you."

Lucina nodded her head, feeling her eyes water. *Pull yourself together*, she chided herself. *Do you want to look like a big baby?*

"You are most welcome to return any time," Señora Labotta continued. "This is your home, always." Lucina hugged her host good-bye, thanking her repeatedly for her kindness and generosity. She picked up her bags, fighting the rising emotions, and followed Teleo to the car.

"Luci," Teleo murmured as they neared the car. "Are you certain you don't want to become my personal assistant?"

Lucina threw her bags on the back seat, looked up at him, lightly hit his arm and then grinned. Teleo already knew the answer, she knew that.

Señora Labotta leaned against the banister on her veranda, arms crossed. Lucina took one last look at her, waved and for the tenth time expressed her thanks for her hospitality. Señora

Labotta waved her away, smiling.

"You can come back anytime, señorita, provided that you weed my garden without complaint and that you cook for me some Canadian food next time!"

Teleo and Lucina climbed into the black pick-up Ford truck, and as Teleo pulled away, Lucina took one long last look at the small little house flooded by early morning sunlight.

Tears fell down her cheeks.

*   *   *

The drive to the airport was mostly silent.

Teleo and Lucina arrived at the airport terminal a little before 9 a.m., two hours before the flight to Montreal. He helped her unload her luggage and they walked side by side into the busy terminal. Seeing a US Airways sign to their left, they slowly made their way to the counter.

After Lucina's seat had been reserved, and her vegetarian meal had been reserved due to Teleo's insistence, Lucina and Teleo walked over to gate 23.

She turned to look at him, feeling dizzy suddenly.

"So, I hope that we hear from you soon," he said, with his warm smile. His eyes glistened and Lucina felt the familiar fire crawl up her back. Not knowing how to thank him, she gave him a hug. His strong arms closed in on her and she felt herself enveloped by a known energy. Her eyes closed and she began to feel like she was drifting down a stream she had never entirely known before.

Teleo pulled back, winking at Lucina.

"I swore an oath to the cave gods I would respect you. Did I do well?"

Lucina laughed and assured him that he had behaved like a true gentleman.

"I'll give you news soon," she said with a forced grin.

"No rush," he replied, straightening up and clearing his throat. He looked hesitant, as though he wanted to tell her something.

"Well, good-bye, until next time," she said slowly.

"Yes, *hasta pronto chica.* Take care of yourself, all right?"

Lucina took one last look at Teleo and then picked up her bag. She walked over to where a man was inspecting passports and tickets, feeling Teleo's eyes on her the whole way.

Lucina, what are you doing? a voice shouted in her head. *You are just going to walk away like that? Haven't you been there before?* She stopped and slowly turned back. Teleo was observing her, immobile, his hands in his blue faded jean pockets. Swiftly, he walked over to her and without warning bent down and kissed her on the lips, firmly and confidently. His strong arms encircled her thin waist, giving her no possibility of pulling away.

But Lucina wouldn't have pulled away from his lips; they were too sweet and soft, too enticing, too wonderful.

She wanted them to stay on hers forever.

Part Two
Fearless

Chapter 9

Lucina sat stiffly on the couch and watched the television. Shivering, she pulled the fleece blanket closer to her cold body and stared at the images without feeling. A Jet Li movie was playing on the screen, *Kiss of the Dragon*. She found herself fantasizing about dying due to a needle being shoved into her neck; it would be less painful than what she was feeling at that moment.

A week gone by, and still I feel like crap, she realized. She rubbed her eyes angrily. *No job, no sun, no heat. And no Teleo.*

Looking around her small three and a half apartment, Lucina began to feel as though she were in a bad dream. The sounds of cars honking outside, the blaring tube in front of her, the footsteps of the Russians above her with their two children, the scratching of shovels outside. Nothing made sense. It all seemed so futile, so dry, and so cold.

The phone rang at that moment. Lucina rapidly slammed her finger on the green button.

"Hello?"

"Luci, it's me, Stace! What's up girl? You didn't even call me when you got in a week ago, what's up with you?" her best friend said.

"Oh, yeah, sorry about that, I've been busy, you know, searching for programming jobs and all," Lucina answered, twisting the phone line around her finger. *Liar, liar, pants on fire.*

"All right, so tonight we're going shopping at the Eaton Center, girl. We have to get you into the Christmas spirit. I'm coming to pick you up at 6 p.m., and then we're gonna have some fun, okay?"

"Oh, I don't know, Stace... I'm feeling somewhat... sick today," Lucina replied. She was becoming good at lying. After all, she had told her mother that she was happy to be back home and that wasn't true in the least.

But Stacey insisted, so Lucina caved in and told her that she would be ready in an hour. As she hung up the receiver, she groaned loudly and slouched back down into the faded blue couch. *Shopping is the last thing I want to do,* Lucina thought. *But since I have nothing else to do, I am going to drag myself out of my living room, go into my large, green bedroom and try to look alive.* She got up and went to the washroom.

"What are you looking at?" Lucina said out loud to her reflection in the bathroom mirror.

Tears appeared in the woman's eyes. She angrily splashed cold water on the reflection.

*   *   *

Lucina sat in Stacey's new red Honda civic, with Britney Spears wailing in the speakers. Stacey was driving down Saint-Catherine Street, checking out the guys walking down the street. Snow lightly fell against the windshield, creating a dream-like impression of the busy life. While Stacey babbled about how fantastic the new Spears album was, Lucina felt like spearing the stereo instead of listening to that horrible voice but of course, she didn't say anything to her friend.

As she was climbing out of the car, Lucina's feet sank into a brown puddle of slush. She muttered a "*mierda*" out loud, and then, not caring that her feet were drenched, walked over to where Stacey was waiting for her. The two women entered the mall, avoiding the many children playing in the entrance.

"Here Comes Santa Claus" blared loudly throughout the gigantic, five-storey mall. It was a terrible cacophony; children screamed, old ladies with their electric chairs ran over people's poor feet, glossy-lipped short-skirted girls talked excitedly over their cell phones, and sales people launched into their sales pitches so loud that half the mall could hear them talking. Then, of course, there was the piercing loud music which was on a loop, and if one stayed long enough, one could catch the same song an hour later, maybe even louder this time.

Lucina felt faint all of a sudden.

Stacey took her friend by the arm and led her into the nearest store. Lucina let herself be directed, feeling limp and tired. Once inside the huge clothes store, Lucina took a look around and her eyes fell across a green sweater in the corner of the store. She stared at it for some time, lost in thought, while Stacey walked up and down aisles, pulling things out randomly, not looking at Lucina.

I guess that everything changes, Lucina thought to herself sadly. *I guess that this life here, which I once thought was normal, seems alien now. It seems that the real aliens are these people fretting with their cell phones, bumping into one another without the least apology, screaming at their children, sipping their sixth coffee and thinking about the next one. The real people are the ones I met in Mexico, the ones who smiled, who took their time serving me, who talked to me about the deeper things in life.*

A feeling of exasperation caught hold of her and the familiar feeling of being suffocated mounted into her chest and throat.

"Wow, this shirt is totally awesome! Peww, it's only $75.00? Wow, this is a great deal. Can you hold this for me, Luci, while I try on a few things?" Stacey looked up at her friend smiling, but noticing her friend's pale face, stopped short. "What's wrong?"

Lucina shrugged casually and mentioned that she wasn't feeling like shopping that day. Looking hurt, Stacey put down the clothes and after a few seconds of consideration, suggested they head for the Second Cup instead to have a heart-to-heart talk. The two women left the mall and headed up McGill Avenue in the chilly night. Snowflakes fell rapidly to the icy ground, creating a white blanket on the street. A few minutes later, Lucina and Stacey entered the dimly-lit coffee shop and Lucina chose a secluded corner in the back near ferns. She let herself fall into a chair while Stacey ordered some tea and came back.

"Your favorite: Cappuccino. Now, tell me what's wrong," Stacey implored.

Lucina wasn't certain if Stacey would understand.

"Stacey, I don't know what I'm doing in my life anymore," Lucina said with difficulty, trying to control her emotions. "I mean, this whole city stinks of superficiality, I can't stand this place anymore. I miss the quiet nature, the long walks in the woods, the horses, the tortillas, the wise words of Señora Labotta and Teleo."

Stacey took a sip of her coffee and shook her head in sympathy. Lucina realized it was pointless trying to explain to her friend what had happened to her in Mexico. How could she even begin to put into words her transformation? It was best to change subjects. Lucina asked her how her new job was going, how her boyfriend Simon was, and Stacey was happy to change subjects.

Lucina only partly listened to her friend that night. She was seeing a whole other scene in her mind's eye. She saw Teleo smiling at her against the backdrop of a charming and welcoming yellow house, and felt his hands upon her legs, applying the green mixture to her snakebite. She saw his gleaming eyes the last day when she took the plane back home and felt his warm lips again. She saw a flash of Señora Labotta's penetrating eyes, her long, stringy black hair fluttering in the wind around her bulky body. And the rapids, with its calming, soothing voice.

Stacey and Montreal were miles away.

*   *   *

As Lucina walked back home in the cold December night, she couldn't help but feel as though there were nothing for her anymore in Montreal, or in Canada for that matter. It was as though the whole world had changed right before her eyes, the world with all its glitter and all its metallic glamour. She kicked a piece of ice lying in front of her in anger.

The city life. *What is so exciting about thousands of people everywhere, about noise and air pollution, about stressed-out strangers slamming into you, about taxi drivers that try everything in their power to cut you off when you cross the street?* she reflected. *What is so exciting about being squashed in the metro with smelly, stressed-out workaholics who have no time to give you the time of day? What is so interesting about going to bars where there are drunken idiots trying to have sex with you on the dance floor? What is so...*

In the darkness, a voice interrupted her dark thoughts.

"Please, do you have a quarter? I don't have a job, I don't have anywhere to go," a hoarse voice whispered in the shadows to Lucina's left.

An old thin woman in a torn beaver fur coat emerged from the blackness, her left hand extending up to Lucina's face. On her head was a brightly colored cloth which seemed vaguely familiar to Lucina. Her brown face and her big brown eyes stared straight into Lucina's eyes.

Lucina stopped walking and turned to face the homeless woman. They stood facing each other for a few seconds before Lucina finally spoke to the beggar in Spanish.

"Where are you from?" she asked the poor woman in Spanish.

"You speak Spanish? Oh, how wonderful!" the stranger exclaimed, a bright smile piercing her faded face. "I'm from the Yucatan, a place called Varadero. It's where I was born. My name is Margarita."

"Why are you in the streets?" Lucina questioned her, filled with a strange sense of déjà-vu. Words were not going to fail her this time.

"I'm here because my son moved to Montreal some years ago, I followed him," replied the old woman. "But then one day, he died and he left me no money since he was poor. Now I'm here, begging for money because I have no job. I'm only a poor, old woman who can cook and sow." She held out her hand again.

Lucina reached out and held the beggar's bony, fragile cold hands and looked into her eyes. She felt as though she were standing in front of the most beautiful, most truthful being she had seen since her return from Mexico. The woman only looked at Lucina, shocked that a stranger was holding her hands and talking to her.

"Would you like a warm place to stay tonight?" Lucina sputtered. She was shocked she had just said that out loud. The old woman gaped at her.

"Excuse me?"

"I said, I invite you over, come, let me help you with these bags," Lucina said, bending down to help the woman.

Now you've totally gone off the deep end, a voice whispered in Lucina's head.

Chapter 10

"You did *what?*" Lucina's mother hollered into the receiver the next morning.

Oh no, I shouldn't have told her, Lucina realized. *Now she will go crazy for real.* Lucina's mother continued to rant over the phone, so much so that Lucina finally told her that she had groceries to buy, and hung up. *So much for telling the truth*, Lucina sighed inwardly. *There's no use with certain people: Some people can't handle the truth. It's better for them to continue sleeping, that way the world won't be so threatening.*

Lucina walked back into her living room and smiled when she saw her guest sitting on the couch, sipping a cup of coffee, bundled up in a thick purple nightgown. Lucina asked Margarita whether she wanted something else, but the woman shook her head, giving Lucina a big, warm smile. Lucina felt happy. As she was about to say something to her guest, the phone rang. Lucina picked it up hurriedly, expecting to hear her mother's frantic voice on the other line.

"Hello?" she sighed into the receiver.

"*Hola*, Lucina," said a deep, familiar voice. "Did I wake you?"

Lucina's face lit up, she quickly turned her back to Margarita, and went into her bedroom. Closing the door, she sat down nervously on the side of her bed. *Teleo is on the other end*, she thought, excited to hear his voice. *What will I say to him?*

"How are you this morning?" Teleo asked, his voice soft and inviting.

"Oh, Teleo," Lucina answered, trying to picture his glowing eyes. "I am fine. How are you?" Her face grew hot and her palms became sweaty. She pictured him sitting on the couch looking at the eagle tapestry, passing his hands through his raven hair.

Teleo told her about how he missed her presence and how his mother lacked a personal helper. Lucina laughed, telling him how she was thinking of them also. When he asked her about Montreal, Lucina didn't want to lie. She told him that she was finding the return very hard on the soul and that she missed the jungle, the heat and especially, a few special Mexicans.

They spoke about random things, until Teleo told her that he had to leave to run errands. Lucina was sorry that their conversation could not last longer, but she promised him that she would call back soon. He told her once again how he was thinking a lot about her, and then hung up. Lucina sighed, fell back on her bed and stared up at the ceiling, visualizing Oaxaca.

"How lovely it is to be alone in the world," she said sarcastically to the ceiling above her. "How lovely to have no one around to love you, or hold you, or tell you you're beautiful. I love my life." She then recalled something Doctor Field had told her a few weeks ago.

"When you are depressed, the only thing you should do is keep busy. See people, do things, don't think; thinking only makes it worse," Doctor Field had said. "Depression takes seed in idleness. When you are running around, you never have time to feel sorry for yourself."

Lucina shook her head. *I need to find something to do or else I will go insane. What can I do? What can I do other than wallow in my misery?* She sat up and went out into the living room. There she found her guest watching television with wide eyes. Margarita looked so immersed in the program that Lucina felt she shouldn't disturb her.

"Margarita," Lucina said gently. "I will go out for a while but

I'll be back around six. Help yourself to food in the fridge and don't answer the phone, I have an answering machine." Margarita moved to kiss Lucina's hand, but Lucina pulled her hand away. "Please don't do that."

Margarita smiled a toothless smile and settled back into the comfortable sofa.

*   *   *

Lucina walked out into a bright cold day on December 23rd, and headed out to her old waitressing job near the plateau Mont Royal. Years ago, she had liked to serve people food because it didn't entail a serious relationship with them. She only had to smile, serve them, and they always left a good tip. *I hope they need a cook*, she thought as she entered the subway station. The subway was nearly empty, except for some elderly people carrying groceries and a few teenagers sprawled on benches. Lucina hated being in crowds of people because she always felt like she was suffocating more around people.

When she arrived at the Italian restaurant, she was lucky to find the same owner working at the restaurant. They exchanged the usual banter, and after a few minutes, Lucina asked Madame Dupré if she needed a good Mexican cook. To Lucina's great relief, Madame Dupré admitted that she needed a kitchen helper and agreed to meet Margarita the following day, even though Margarita had no references in Montreal.

"You look good, Luci," Madame Dupré commented.

It's funny how looks are deceiving, Lucina thought as she smiled and promised to return to eat at a later date. *Never rely on appearances.*

Once outside, Lucina had a thought. *I will visit Mr. Steve and make peace with him*, she decided. *I will go to his office, tell him I forgive him for ruining my life when he fired me, and I will tell him I don't hate men anymore, that I just have problems with certain souls.*

She walked to the metro, content that she was finally settling something big in her life.

Sitting in the metro, she noticed a young woman across from her who was applying her lipstick while looking in the reflection of the window. Several men were checking out her slim, tanned legs. Carefully, the woman traced her lower and upper lip with a pencil. Afterwards, she took out a bright pink lip gloss and slowly, using a circular gesture, rubbed the gloss on her lips. She ruffled her hair a bit, smacked her lips together, and to finish, she ran her tongue over her teeth to make sure that they were spotless, and then returned to her original seating arrangement.

Lucina continued to stare at her. A small smile crept up on Lucina's face.

"*Qu'est-ce que tu veux, espèce de... lesbienne?*" the woman snapped at Lucina, picking up her bags quickly. Before she could get up and leave for another bench, Lucina replied.

"*Je me demandais seulement combien de temps par jour tu te maquilles et combien de temps par jour tu penses à ton âme,*" Lucina said with a smile.

The woman stopped dead in her tracks and turned red. Quickly, she stomped over to the next bench and sat down. *Now where did that come from?* Lucina wondered. *I have never said those things out loud before. Words are coming back to me.*

Doctor Field would be proud of me.

*   *   *

Lucina got off at the next metro station, metro Vendôme, and quickly walked to the building where she used to spend most of her time just a few months ago. She looked up at the tall, black brick building and a wave of fear hit her.

What am I going to say to him again? she thought.

When she got to the fifth floor, Lucina fell upon a new secretary who was filing her nails diligently, carefully blowing on her cuticles. The brunette looked up and with a huge white beaming smile asked how she could help Lucina. Lucina responded dryly that she could send for Mr. Steve right away and tell him that Lucina Pilano was waiting to see him. The secretary fluttered away, leaving Lucina standing in the grand entrance of NewI. Unsure of what to do, she decided to sit down on the comfortable black leather sofa near the huge eight feet aquarium and to pick up the first magazine next to her.

Randomly, she opened a page and read the title: *New-Age Men*. She selected a random passage.

Remember we are not in medieval Times anymore: There are no more knights in shining armor.

Maybe this will be enriching, she thought, amused and curious.

Nowadays, women are more independent than ever before in history. They have jobs, and have powerful positions in society. Women are no longer dependent on men, and men are losing their traditional bread-winner roles. What is a man to do in this world? A man must re-evaluate his position and become equal to women. If he remains in the old medieval mentality, no woman will truly desire him.

Women want new-age men. What is a new-age man? A new-age man is a man who realizes he should let his woman be all that she is inside. He should let her work as hard as him, and as long as him. He should aid in the housework and aid in child-rearing. A new-age man should stand by his woman and tell her, "Shine, shine, and shine some more! For many centuries you have been repressed, and now you must shine."

Men, you must re-evaluate your roles. Remember that

*women are changing faster than you can imagine. Women
will no longer remain idle, cooking-cleaning house-wives.
We are reaching the top, and if you cannot adapt to our
changes, then you will be left behind. Why so many divorces?
Because women know now they can make it on their own,
they are strong now, they have money, power and education.
What do we need medieval men for? To drag us back down
into history...*

The secretary fluttered back into the office and smiled at Lucina,
awkwardly. Lucina put the article down and stood up quickly.

"Mr. Steve is busy right now, but he..." she began.

"Right, of course he's busy right now," Lucina replied loudly.
The secretary stood still, on guard.

"I have an idea, something that might work," Lucina said.
Walking over to the blinking camera opposite from her, she
stood right underneath the flashing red light. "Well, Mr. Steve,
knowing you, you will be watching this as we speak. I recall it
was a habit of yours during your lunch to observe clients coming
in. Since you can't come out to face me, I guess I'll have to face
this blinking machine instead. I've come to tell you that I don't
hate you anymore, that I understand that you are an ignorant soul
who happens to be in a male shell. I have also realized (since you
fired me and stole my invention), that working in computers just
doesn't cut it for me anymore. I want something more...alive in
my life. Good-bye then."

As the secretary stood gaping at her, Lucina turned on her
heel, walked towards the door marked *Sortie* and pushed the
heavy door.

Well, Doctor Field, you would be proud of me, she thought happily. *I finally stood up for myself, and expressed myself. For once, I did
what was good for me and not what was good for others.*

*   *   *

The next morning, Margarita went for her job interview. She had scribbled a few words down in Spanish, telling Lucina how grateful and happy she was that God had brought her into her life. On the stove was a pan filled with eggs, beans and rice. Lucina picked up a fork and dug into the sweet-smelling Mexican breakfast.

At that moment, the phone rang and Lucina answered it. Mrs. Pilano was calling her daughter to ask her at what time she would be over for supper the following day. Lucina brought her hands to her forehead and gasped: She had totally forgotten about Christmas! Thank God she had already bought her mother a gift in Mexico. She told her mother 5 p.m., and told her that she was bringing someone special over.

"Lucina! Don't do this to me!" her mother implored. "I don't want a beggar in my house for Christmas. Please, reconsider; this is not a homeless shelter!"

Lucina groaned and told her mother that for the love of her God, that she could at least show some mercy on Christmas. Mrs. Pilano was silent, and after a few seconds of silence, in a dramatic voice she told her daughter that Margarita was welcomed.

Christmas is the worst example of we-are-good-Christians syndrome ever, Lucina noted to herself. *While there are poor homeless people freezing their butts off in the streets, we sit at home and sing "Hallelujah" over and over again. As if singing will change anything. Then we hand over paper bags filled with canned foods to poor families, thinking that this gesture makes up for all the other selfishness of the year. We give a dollar to the homeless man on Christmas day, and he smiles, and we smile, and that's the end of our compassion. Christmas is superficial and so are we,* Lucina concluded, shaking her head.

Walking over to the sink, she began washing the dishes. Cars honked outside, the kids stomped like wild elephants upstairs, and the radio next door blared a hip-hop song, something about killing a girl and putting her in a trunk of a car. *God save me*, Lucina thought. *God save me. What world is this that I am living in?*

There was a sudden silence. Stunned that silence had hit, Lucina stopped doing the dishes and crept up to the window. Looking outside, she noticed tiny white snowflakes falling gently across the Montreal streets. The children had stopped stomping upstairs, the radio song had vanished and the cars had melted away.

Looking down on the sidewalk, Lucina's eyes widened. A few words had been written on the white sidewalk right under her window. She took a second to read the words and gasped. There, on the snowy sidewalk, were written the words "Follow your heart". Lucina stared and stared at those words for a long time, forgetting the running water in the sink. She glanced around to see if she could recognize anyone near the apartment outside, but no one was in sight.

Slowly, she made her way back to the sink, closed the faucet and blinked rapidly. She wandered over to the sofa and sank into the blue cushions.

Follow your heart.

What on earth is going on? Is Stacey playing a joke on me? Or maybe Margarita wrote those words? Lucina thought in bewilderment. She sat and stared out the window for a long while. Images of mountains, rivers, horses, sunshine, palm trees, and giant white birds flashed before her eyes. She heard the sound of the rapids swishing past her, the sound of Kaila and Kailo's drum in the night air, the sound of birds chirping in the jungle.

Follow your heart.

She saw the tiny *pueblo* of smiling Mexicans, the grinning boy who had greeted her one morning in the park as she was writing in her diary. She saw the smile across Señora Labotta's face as she spoke to her of love.

Follow your heart.

She felt Teleo's warm hands on her body, telling her of their power to transcend with their bodies. She recalled the soft cotton sheets in Señora Labotta's bed as she lay with a high fever. She remembered the snake bite as it spread like wild fire up her leg, and the feeling of dizziness as she lay in Teleo's arms.

"What is it about that place that makes me feel so at home?" she asked out loud. "Is it the weather, the sun, the jungle, or the people?" The answer came to her swiftly: People. They made life a living hell or a paradise. Sartre had been right when he had stated, "*L'enfer, c'est les autres*".

"I am surrounded by superficial, empty shells! No wonder I am depressed. I need to find a place where I am with my own species and certainly not computers. No more computers. How long have I been dead in this society? How long?" Lucina said angrily to the walls around her.

The noise of the screaming baby upstairs rushed back, hip hop came blasting back, along with the cars honking, the thudding upstairs and the constant bustle on the sidewalk of people rushing to work. Lucina stood up abruptly and took a look around the once-cozy apartment. Suddenly, she felt like kicking everything and burning her apartment.

Hurriedly, she walked over to her closet and pulled the doors open. *All these clothes!* she thought with frustration. *What are all these clothes to me? I don't need these things if I'm miserable. My mother is a religious freak who can't think for herself, always needing a Bible to define her reality and running to church whenever she has a breakdown. My best friend is a superficial ditz, who has no idea what being alive means. Everyone's eyes are empty, their speech is empty. The only thing which people love is money and look what money does, it makes them unhappy. Locke was right: Property only causes injury.*

Lucina stomped around her room furiously, trying to calm herself. She was shaking as though she had been bitten by the coral snake again. This time, only coldness spread in her veins.

"What is going on? Why am I so upset? Why can't I just be happy with all these things, like everyone else?" she screamed out loud. "What makes my life in Mexico so appealing compared to my life here?"

The phone rang.

"Hello!" she yelled into the receiver.

An automated voice responded.

"Hello, we are the Professional Cleaners Pro Company, calling to tell you how you can save this season with our new inexpensive carpet cleaner teams. For only $19.99 you can have an estimation…"

In a fit of rage, Lucina threw the phone across her room and lay down across her bed. *God, oh God, what am I going to do?* she thought. *I don't want to be a machine anymore. I want to feel life, I want to live life.*

She stood up and looked around her bedroom, her body convulsing. She knew what she had to do: She had to change her life, and drastically change it.

"Well, Luci, there's only one thing to do: Leave this place," she said to the emptiness around her. "It's time to move on, to move out of this fake plastic society and move into the jungle, where people still follow their hearts, dance around fires, and where there is a wonderful man waiting for me."

She reached inside her closet and pulled out all the suitcases she owned.

Now, how many suitcases does one need when one is moving to another country? she mused, scratching her head. She decided to Google her question.

Chapter 11

It's incredible how much one can accomplish when one is no longer afraid of people's judgments, afraid of the past, afraid of making mistakes. Lucina realized that day that she was no longer going to let fear guide her. She wanted to start a new life, one that would only be led by her heart. Teleo had been right in saying that it was easier to fall into the pit of fear than climb the mountain of love. She had been in the pit her whole life, depending on others to find happiness. Now she was going to step out of her miserable hole and live her life fully, go all the way to the end of the world if need be. She was going to be alive.

On Christmas day, with Margarita sitting next to her, Lucina told her mother that she was leaving for another country for an indeterminate time. Shocked, Mrs. Pilano dropped her fork on the floor and stared at her daughter from across the mahogany table. Margarita murmured something in Spanish and left the table while Lucina quietly looked at her mother, and put her hands upward as a sign of surrender.

Regaining her senses, Mrs. Pilano got up from her seat and told her daughter that she was insane, that she deserved to be locked up in a mental asylum for thinking such crazy thoughts. She cried that Lucina had truly lost her mind now, that losing her job and Lincoln had just been the beginning of her delusion. She lamented that Lucina was certainly going to regret moving to Mexico if she went, and that she would be abandoning her own mother in Montreal, all alone in the world.

Lucina sat through the tantrum for a while, until at long last, when she saw that her mother was getting tired, she decided to venture a few words.

"Mom, sit down. I am moving to Mexico because I don't feel at home here anymore. I can't stand the flakiness of it all, the fake people, the fake jobs, the fake happiness. I want something real; do you understand what this means, real? I want to feel things, I want to share things, I want to return to nature and feel the ground. I don't want to freeze my ass off anymore in winter. I want the sun, the wind and the freedom of not having to conform. I want something new, and I won't have that here. I will move to Mexico and nothing you or anyone else will say can change my mind."

Mrs. Pilano stared at Lucina and shakily reached for her wine glass. After finishing it off rapidly, she put her head down in her hands, said a few prayers to her Lord and looked up at Lucina, tears in her eyes.

"Luci, I can't believe you're doing this, but if this is what you want, I can't keep you from leaving," Mrs. Pilano blurted out emotionally. "So, I hope that you will find happiness where you're going, and for the sake of Jesus, Mary, Joseph, Saint Andrew, Saint Matthew..."

"Mom, I get the point," Lucina sighed. *I knew this was going to be tough,* she thought. *But does she always have to be so dramatic about everything?*

Margarita ventured back to the table and soon after, Christmas began with its Christmas songs and egg nog. Mrs. Pilano lit a fire in the chimney and the three women sat silently watching the flames leap into the dark chimney. By the end of the evening, Lucina's mother had drunk half the bottle of wine and had even sung some Christian songs to accompany Margarita on the piano. Lucina looked at Margarita and was in awe of her change. A few days ago, Margarita had been a homeless woman with no mittens in the cold streets of Montreal, and there she was now, laughing and playing piano, as if there were nothing the matter in the world.

This is Christmas, Lucina thought happily. *This is how it should be done all the time. Jesus would be proud of us. The real Jesus, not the one in the Bible,* she reminded herself.

At two o'clock in the morning, Margarita and Mrs. Pilano hugged each other, and once more, Lucina invited Margarita back to her apartment. On the way home, the old woman kept repeating how her life had changed since she had met her. Lucina told her that her own life had changed very recently and that she was most grateful to be able to help another. The two new friends hugged, after wishing each other Merry Christmas again, and then Lucina walked into her green bedroom, closed the door and lay down on the Queen sized-bed, hands behind her head. She looked up at the grey ceiling, and smiled.

She closed her eyes and for the first time in over a week, Lucina began to really think of Teleo.

*   *   *

On Boxing Day, Lucina got up earlier than usual and found that Margarita had already left for her new kitchen job. She called the airline company to reserve a one way ticket for the following day destination Mexico City, December 27th, at 6:45 a.m. She punched in her credit card number, and once the flight was confirmed, hung up the phone.

One day left before takeoff, she reflected. *What does a person do when they have one day left of their old life and one day left before a new life begins?*

Lucina reached for the phone and called Stacey. She knew that it would be hard for her friend to understand, so it was better to do this sort of thing over the phone. Stacey's voice came through. Lucina patiently and gently explained that she would be moving to Mexico for a few months, and that she wasn't sure when she would be returning to Montreal.

"My God, Luci, you're leaving for real?" Stacey whispered. "I mean, we've known each other for so long, what am I going to do without you? I was just telling Simon how grateful I am for having such a close friend like you."

Lucina remained silent, not sure that she knew how to say good-bye. Stacey told her that she would call Lucina every week in Mexico and that she would write to her over internet. Lucina laughed and told her that she would make it to an internet café just for her. The two friends continued talking for some time then Lucina excused herself, promising to keep in touch.

Looking around her small but tidy bedroom, Lucina reasoned that she would only bring the essentials, and that the rest she would leave behind. She took out three suitcases, started piling in old photo albums, diaries, letters, favorite clothes, a few CD's, and some bathroom accessories. She would ship the rest of her belongings later by boat, it would be less expensive.

After she had finished packing, she called her mother, explained to her that she would be leaving the following day, and mentioned that she really needed her to sign the subletting contract to her apartment.

"Who will rent your apartment, dear? I can't stay in it, I already have a place!"

Lucina reassured her mother, and told her not to worry about because she already had someone in mind.

Margarita returned home a few hours later, told her host that she had really enjoyed cooking again, and said that she felt the boss had appreciated her. Lucina was happy to learn she had been accepted at her old job. Unsure of how to approach the following subject, Lucina decided not to beat around the bush.

"Margarita. I am moving to Mexico and I would like to lease

my apartment to you, providing of course that you make the pay-
ments and you take care of this place while I am gone," Lucina
said.

Margarita turned white. She dropped her bags and grabbed
Lucina`s hand.

"Señorita, are you kidding me? Is this a joke?" Margarita
asked, becoming pale.

Lucina shook her head, dead serious.

"If you tell me that you do this because you are leaving for
real, then I will accept. But I will owe you so much, I will never
forget all that you have done for me," Margarita said with great
emotion, putting her hand over her heart and crying.

"Margarita, I am serious, and I want you to have this apartment. I know you will take care of things here. I have no one else
who can take it on such short notice. But I want you to promise
me you will keep that job and work hard."

Margarita was speechless.

"I don't know what to say…"

"Just say thank you," Lucina murmured, taking her hands in
hers. "Someone recently also changed my life, and I want to give
you the same chance that person gave me. So let's take care of
this subletting contract."

*   *   *

An hour later, Mrs. Pilano arrived, dressed in black, as though
she were going to a funeral. Lucina hugged her mother, shaking
her head.

"Mom, do you always have to be so dramatic? This isn't a
funeral!" Lucina exclaimed, unhappily. Her mother snorted and
didn't respond.

The three women walked into the elevator together in silence. Lucina pressed the sixth floor button while looking at both

of the women out of the corner of her eye. Mrs. Pilano clutched
her cross with both hands, her lower lip trembled slightly, her
greyish short hair hung loose around her shoulders, and her black
woollen shawl hugged her slightly over-weight body. Lucina
stared down at her mother's boots, realizing that she was still
wearing the same boots as ten years ago: Big, black Sorel boots
with fake white wool trim.

Next to Mrs. Pilano, Margarita looked fragile and small and
white. She wore a blue sweater Lucina had given her, with a long,
brown nylon skirt. Her face was wrinkled with time, her mouth
thinned by years of suffering. *What this woman has lived, I can't
begin to understand,* Lucina thought sadly. *At least I can help her
in some way.*

When they arrived on the sixth floor, Lucina walked over to
645, and knocked loudly. A short scruffy-looking man opened
the door an inch, giving them a rude look.

"Oui?"

*"Bonjour, monsieur Lafleur, je viens pour sous-louer mon ap-
partement. Voici ma mère et la femme qui va sous-louer. "*

Monsieur Lafleur looked somewhat surprised that Lucina
wanted to sublet her apartment so unexpectedly but opened the
door anyway. A strong whiff of cigar invaded Lucina's nostrils.
Monsieur Lafleur led the three women over to his dimly-lit office to the left, stepped over a few beer cases scattered on the
floor and muttered under his breath. He shuffled some papers,
and finally, finding what it was he was looking for, looked over
to Margarita.

"I understand you vant to take over the *logement* of Ms. Pilano?" monsieur Lafleur said in Quebecois English.

"Yes, I do," Margarita replied, almost in a whisper.

"Hmm. What are your *références?*"

"Umm, monsieur Lafleur, Margarita is a...family friend,"
Lucina piped in. "My mother will vouch for her, if there is a
problem, you can contact my mother anytime."

Monsieur Lafleur grunted something inaudible in French, handed the papers over to Mrs. Pilano who shakily signed her name in several places.

"Where you from?" monsieur Lafleur asked Margarita, as he lit a cigar.

"Mexico, señor."

Monsieur Lafleur smiled, banging his fists on his desk.

"*Ah, le Mexique! Quelle belle place. J'adore le Mexique.* Good people, nice people. Velcome to your new home!"

Lucina couldn't help but grin. *Ah, Montrealers are so welcoming,* she thought with amusement. *The minute they hear that someone is from another country, they nearly jump on them.*

*   *   *

That evening, Lucina took Margarita out to an expensive vegetarian restaurant on the plateau. They ate delicious salads with organic carrot soup and home-made apple pie, and talked in Spanish. Lucina had a fit of laughing during the evening and nearly choked on a celery stick. Margarita looked up with glittering eyes, staring at her host with fascination.

"Why are you laughing?" she asked her.

"I am laughing because no one will believe me if I tell them what I am about to do. They will think I have gone off the deep end," Lucina answered, trying to stop her crazy laughter.

"The deep end?"

"Oh, it means to go crazy."

Margarita leaned over and smiled her toothless smile.

"Señorita, this world is crazier than us. Look how people live. All they do is suffer endlessly, and there is nothing anyone does to help. That to me is crazy."

Lucina nodded, plunging into her own contemplations of suffering. It was time to move on, to bury the hatchet. She didn't want to remain on the cross her whole life.

Chapter 12

Lucina dragged her heavy suitcases across to the counter, handed her passport over to a blond woman who quickly punched some figures into her computer, smiling. A voice inside of Lucina was dying to get out, so she gave in and spoke her mind.

"Excuse me, do you enjoy working on that computer all day?" she asked the woman.

"What?" answered the blond, with a puzzled look on her face.

"I asked if you enjoyed working on your computer all day."

"Oh, well, you know, my eyes get tired sometimes but you get used to it. Everyone works with computers now, it's the twenty-first century," the young woman replied, almost scolding.

Lucina nodded sympathetically, trying to remind herself that once she too had been blinded by a dull screen all day. The blond gave her back her papers, wished Lucina a good trip and then turned to the next client. Diligently, Lucina loaded all three of her suitcases on the rolling carpet and then turned to walk with her mother.

"Oh, Luci!" Mrs. Pilano exclaimed, clutching her cross. "I have been praying for your soul. I just hope that your plane won't get bombed by some terrorist group or something. Please, just be careful of those, you know...people with turbans."

"Mother, can you please stop being racist?" Lucina sighed, holding her mother by the arm. "We have talked about this a thousand times, you know that I don't buy what they sell in the media. Now, I want us to enjoy this time together until I board the plane, and please don't be so freaken dramatic!"

Lucina's mother sighed. *It is her Italian blood making her so dramatic,* Lucina reminded herself. *It's blood, what can one do?*

Mother and daughter slowly made their way over to the airport coffee shop. Lucina picked out a small table near the center and her mother sat down, looking lost in the crowd of tourists. They ordered two cappuccinos and one croissant. Lucina knew the plane food was going to be disgusting, so she decided to eat before taking off.

"Luci, I just don't understand. If your father were still here, he would have never approved. These Mexicans, who knows what their intentions are? But I know," Mrs. Pilano said, seeing Lucina frown, "This means a lot to you, so I will pray for you each night. And you have to call me, and if you ever feel like coming home again, you always have a place with me."

"Thanks mom, I know," Lucina replied, taking a sip of her coffee.

This is what happens when you flow and let go, Lucina thought. *I should be blaming Doctor Field, it was his advice to begin with. He always told me to flow like water, so here I am, a waterfall out of control.*

But at least I am alive.

"You know Luci, when you were a little girl you were always so sporadic. I could never tell what you would do next. Once you were playing outside in the winter time and you decided to take off your boots and run in the snow. I was so mortified, do you remember? I ran downstairs, grabbed you and yelled at you. Are you leaving because I used to yell at you?" Mrs. Pilano asked, her lips trembling.

Lucina shook her head and sighed. She took her mother's hands and pressed them.

"Mother, some things are just not about you, you know? They are about me."

Mrs. Pilano smiled, tears in her eyes.

"That's good to know, my child, that you are not leaving because of your old mother. I could never bear it, knowing you hate me."

An automated voice interrupted her lamentation.

"Flight 465, Mexico City, is now boarding at terminal 5. All passengers please go to the gate for boarding."

"Mom, I should be going now, but I need to ask you a favor before I leave," Lucina said, looking serious. "I need you to take care of Margarita for me, you know, call her often like you do for me and see if she needs help. It is of utmost importance that she is cared for, this woman deserves it. No one deserves to live on the streets and Montreal should be caring for such people instead of giving them pocket money. Promise me, mother?"

"Luci, I will take care of her, since it's your wish," her mother replied, wiping her wet eyes with her napkin.

They got up slowly, Lucina taking her mother in her arms.

"Thank you, mom, for understanding me. Maybe I'm doing what all people should be doing: Pursuing their heart's wishes. I'm scared to death, but I don't care anymore: I need to do this."

Lucina walked away without looking back. Looking back meant that she might never have the courage to move forward, so she kept right on walking, through the sliding doors of terminal 5.

*   *   *

On the plane, she sat next to a strange, thin elderly man who was jotting words down on a faded yellow sheet of paper, and often massaging his neck with vigor. The weirdest thing he kept doing was humming an annoying song which sounded very much like the song "Somewhere over the Rainbow".

Lucina stared out the little oval window, trying to catch a glimpse of the Pierre Elliot Trudeau airport. The sun was about to rise and she was hoping to catch the first rays of light. Suddenly, the man turned and looked intensely at her, his brown eyes wide with excitement.

"I'm inventing something right as we speak, miss, so I would ask you not to interfere with my invention!"

Lucina was stunned.

"I won't bother you. I'm not doing anything," she replied, somewhat aggravated. Curiosity got the better of her. "May I ask what you are inventing?"

"Yes, you may. I'm inventing a new language. It's called Telepathy, and you might have heard of it," he answered, studying Lucina closely.

Lucina gaped at him. She responded that as far as she knew, telepathy had already been invented. The man scoffed at her and shook his head, explaining that the notion had been invented but not the *real* technique. Lucina didn't know what to reply, so she decided to ask him what she was thinking about, just for fun. The thin man squeezed his eyes shut and then, several seconds later, he opened them again. He had a strange look on his face.

"You are moving to another country!" he said dramatically. Lucina was stunned. Surely her mother had put him up to this. She decided to test him further: Her mother didn't know about Teleo or about his strange mother.

"Am I meeting someone over there?" Lucina asked him.

"Yes you are. Two people who love you very much," responded the man. Lucina turned to look at him and frowned. *This is impossible,* she thought. *My mother has paid this man to put fears into me. I can't believe she would do this to me.*

"How did you do that?" Lucina demanded. "Has my mother put you up to this?"

"Your mother? I don't know your mother. But to answer your question on how I did that, I will explain to you. It's a procedure, a simple procedure which takes time and effort. I've been working on this ever since I was very young. I won't tell you all the formula, but the first step is to turn off your inner dialogue, you know, the little voices in your head."

Lucina nodded her head, staring at him, incredulous that she was even having such a conversation. The strange man continued massaging his neck with great energy.

"You turn off the voices, and then, you focus all your attention on the other person in front of you. Eventually, you focus your attention so much on that person that you begin to feel that person as though you were them."

"You mean, you sort of become the other person?" Lucina questioned, curious. *Maybe this is for real,* she realized.

"Something like that. You become *more* than yourself. But this formula only works if you forget about your voices, remember that. Now, wait, let me see, what your name is, Lily? Loni? Wait, wait. Laila. Luci! Hello, my name is Walter, Walter Kepps. Nice to meet you on this lovely aircraft!"

They shook hands. Lucina was certain that her mother had arranged this meeting, but she continued to play along. Curious, she asked Walter more about himself and he explained that he had lived his whole life in the north of Quebec, near the little town of Charlevoix. He had started to take interest in telepathy when he had begun to notice that his cats always sensed strangers arriving at his home before they actually arrived. Walter had deducted that animals had a more developed sixth sense due to their weaker mental activity, and concluded that the only thing preventing humans from accessing their telepathic powers was their big brain or the Tormentor as he called it.

"The Tormentor is just what it is: It torments the living hell out of us. When we are supposed to be enjoying ourselves, there It is, always making us think about stupid little things. Animals don't have that. Have you ever seen an animal stop, think, before launching into pursuit of a squirrel or bunny or beetle? No! Animals just act. With this gift, they can feel things around them much more than us. For instance, we all know that animals act up before a storm. They feel electricity in the air, and react to it. We are also supposed to act up before a storm but the Tormentor is always there."

Lucina asked him how it felt to know what others were thinking all the time. She really wanted to catch him off guard, in order to expose him as an impostor. Walter explained that he could turn off his gift when he wanted and just stare at people, but the minute he focused on others, then he could read their thoughts.

"In the future, people will be born with this gift. It is inevitable that the human race will evolve into telepathic beings," Walter explained to Lucina. "Even you have it. The feeling that you have when you think of someone out of the blue, for example, that is a form of telepathy. You're watching television, and bang, there is a vision of your best friend. And the next minute, she calls you. Coincidence? Never. We just have to pay more attention to these flashes and eventually, when the Tormentor is silenced, you will really read other people's thoughts."

At that moment, the flight attendant walked by and gave them a weird look.

"You see her? She just thought that we're a bunch of freaks because we're talking about telepathy. People think it's all Star Trek shit. But it's not! It's a few years away, ready to hatch."

Lucina smiled at him. *Well,* she reflected, *he might just be a loony after all. Maybe my mother had nothing to do with this.*

Walter returned to scribbling something on his yellow paper. After a few minutes he looked up, grinning.

"Here's a thought for you. The next time you feel something, automatically say it out loud, as crazy as it sounds to you. The Tormentor won't be able to act as quickly to interfere. Here, I'll demonstrate," he said. He shut his eyes tightly, took several deep breaths and then leaned all the way back in his seat. All of a sudden, his eyes opened wide and he yelled, "Snake come and wake me! Fire is the source of life! Fright go away, and fire come again!"

Lucina turned pale. People turned around, staring and frowning. Her mouth dropped open. *Oh my God,* she thought. *I have entered the* Twilight Zone *again and this time, it's not on foreign ground. I must have a few screws loose for real.*

"See, how it works," Walter said excitedly. "I tried to read your mind, and then these strange words came to me. Does it make any sense to you?"

Lucina shook her head and turned away, pretending that he had said nonsense. However, deep inside, she was shaken. Fire, why did it always have to do with fire?

There are things on this planet that I will never get, she concluded, sighing.

*   *   *

Their plane arrived in Mexico City at 1:32 p.m. Lucina shook hands with Walter Kepps, promising to keep a look out for his upcoming book on telepathy, and he wished her good luck with adapting to a new country.

"Remember, a good yelp once in while will shut that Tormentor for good!" he reminded Lucina, as they walked off the plane.

Lucina nodded and walked away. *Nod and smile,* she told herself. *Nod and smile.*

Once in the crowded luggage retrieval area, she picked out her three heavy suitcases, and asked a young Mexican boy to assist her in taking them to the taxi area. From there, Lucina flagged a taxi and gave directions to the bus terminal, where she had to wait two hours before the next bus to Oaxaca. Hungry and tired, she sat down in the waiting area and looked at Mexican television for some time, trying to distract herself. By 4 p.m., she was seated on a bus with many other Spanish families, heading towards Oaxaca. She fell asleep quickly and had a vivid dream.

She was on a large sailing boat, surrounded by dozens of women who were all of different ages. Each one was busy doing something different; one was calculating numbers, one was writing on a board, one was singing, and another dancing. Then, Lucina saw a young girl in the corner of the boat, crying. No one was paying attention to her. Her brown hair was dishevelled, and she looked dirty.

"Why are you crying?" Lucina asked her, bending down to look at her.

"I'm crying because I don't know what I'm doing here," the child answered, tears streaming down her face. Lucina reached inside her bag, handed her a brown leather notebook, and watched as the girl happily snatched it and ran off on the deck. Impulsively, Lucina walked over to the side of the boat and looked down into the dark waters. In front of her appeared a little elf swimming in the dark waters who seemed to be waving at her. Lucina waved back. He kept waving.

"Be fearless!" he yelled.

Lucina looked around her. The women had disappeared, as well as the little girl. She was alone on the big ship, looking into the tumultuous waters.

"Be fearless!"

Lucina took a long look again at the water, and although she was afraid, she closed her eyes and let herself fall into the ocean. There was a loud sound as she hit the water.

Awakened by the sound of screeching tires, Lucina opened her eyes. The dream still felt very real to her. Darkness surrounded her. People were poking their heads above the seats, looking around, speaking rapidly in Spanish. The bus had come to a full stop on the side of the road.

"*Que está pasando?*" Lucina asked a woman next to her. The woman didn't reply, she simply rolled her eyes and began praying. The bus driver was speaking into the microphone in rapid Spanish.

"Please, people, no panic. All is under control. There are two armed men in front of my bus, please remain calm, nothing will happen to anybody if you all remain calm."

A few women started praying out loud to Mary, babies began crying, and a man kicked the seat in front of him angrily. Lucina sat straight up in her seat, and for the first time in a while, started thinking that perhaps her mother had been right: Mexico might be more dangerous than she had originally thought.

The doors opened and two men dressed in army clothes, carrying rifles, stepped into the bus. One was a tall, tough-looking, muscular man wearing a face mask; the other was shorter and somewhat plump.

"Nobody move! We're not going to hurt you, we just want your money and your valuables, so if you co-operate, everything will be fine!" the taller one shouted in Spanish.

A few women around Lucina started wailing. She tried to act as though she was not afraid, but inside of her, her stomach performed somersaults. What had Señora Labotta said to her a while back about death? That she shouldn't worry about death, that she should worry about life? That she was young and had more to live?

"God, I hope that she was right. I don't want to die now, not now," Lucina whispered to herself. The men grabbed people's jewelry and stuffed the valuables into heavy army bags, their rifles aimed in people's faces. When they came to Lucina's seat, she handed over her gold earrings, and around $100.00 US. The men didn't ask her for her wallet and Lucina was relieved because she had much more money in her wallet than in her pockets.

After they had done their rounds, the robbers yelled something Lucina didn't understand in Spanish and took off into the night with their army bags. The bus door was left opened, the humid air rushed inside, and the only sound Lucina heard was the soft rain against the window pane.

"This happens almost every time I take the bus," the woman said next to Lucina. She looked almost bored. The bus driver settled back into his seat, took the microphone again, and asked if everyone was all right. A few people talked angrily in Spanish.

"Can't something be done about such things?" Lucina asked the woman next to her, shocked that she had just lived through a hold-up.

"Nothing, señorita. The police are probably the ones stealing from us, so there's no point. Plus they can't set up security everywhere along these roads at night. I always keep my money hidden in my underwear, that way, they can't steal it."

Lucina took a long breath of fresh air which was coming in through the opened doors and stared out the window, noticing the silhouettes of menacing trees and shrubs. The rest of the bus ride was a gloomy one. The gold earrings had been a present from her mother six years ago; Lucina had received them after finishing cegep, and ever since then, she had worn them for good-luck.

What bad luck, she thought miserably. *I hope this doesn't mean that I made a wrong choice in coming here.*

Chapter 13

Early the next morning, the bus arrived in Oaxaca. Trying to contain her excitement, Lucina stepped off the bus and immediately went to the man who was looking for people's suitcases beneath the bus and gave him the description of her three suitcases. The Mexican slowly rummaged underneath the bus, and every minute or so, he would pull out a suitcase and raise an eyebrow. Lucina would shake her head vigorously. Exasperated, she told him that she would find them herself and poked around under the bus until she retrieved all three suitcases.

After hailing a taxi, she asked the cab driver to drive her to *78 Calle de los Aves.* Once in the beat-up Toyota Corolla, the man asked his client what she was doing in Mexico, and when Lucina told him that she was moving there permanently, the cab driver looked shocked.

"Why you move here, when in Canada you have so much nice things? So much nice people, so much nice country! Here, it poor, it have no good government, no good police, no good wages, everything in poor condition. You crazy?"

Lucina remained silent, staring out the window. Finally, she answered. "Yes, I think I'm crazy, but at least I'm not afraid anymore. I want to live." The man looked confused, shrugged, and turned the radio on.

Lucina understood that he hadn't understood her at all.

Twenty minutes later, the taxi pulled up into a familiar driveway. Lucina smiled, gave the man a gracious tip, dragged her suitcases over to the sagging porch, and stood them up next to the tiny table with the timid golden eyes. Breathless with excitement and anticipation, Lucina knocked on the door, barely able to contain her joy. Would Teleo open the door, mop in hand, his glowing green eyes glinting in the early morning sunlight? Would his mother come with a cup of tea, a blue shawl sprawled across her thick shoulders, her stringy black hair tied in a bun?

Lucina knocked again, this time louder. There was no answer. She leaned against the wall, closing her eyes.

Maybe I should have called before coming here, Lucina realized, fear creeping into her stomach.

*   *   *

Four hours and a half later, Lucina heard an old beat-up truck pull up in the unpaved driveway. She opened her eyes just in time to see Señora Labotta step out of the truck, carrying groceries, mumbling to herself. When she saw Lucina, she stopped, blinked and then a large smile appeared on her face. Señora Labotta didn't seem surprised to see her old guest.

"So, you have come back, I was sure you would return, but so soon?" Señora Labotta said, putting her groceries on the small table and giving Lucina a strong hug.

"Hello, Señora!" Lucina replied, grinning. "I'm so glad to be back here. I thought that I might move into the neighborhood, you know, try a little something new." She hoped she didn't look as foolish as she felt.

Señora Labotta laughed uproariously.

"So, now you are all in the heart and the head has stopped functioning, you have hit the other end of the scale I see," Señora Labotta said, patting Lucina's arm. "Well, it takes time to adjust to living in the heart. I give you credit, though, for making the move. Congratulations."

Lucina forced a laugh, putting her arms up in surrender.

"My mother thinks I have gone off the deep end," she replied.

Señora Labotta shook her head and smiled. After helping Lucina with her luggage, the Mexican invited Lucina to sit down on the couch while she prepared some cold iced tea. Lucina was exhausted by that time and happy to ingest some caffeine.

"I'm sorry to say this," Señora Labotta called from the kitchen, "But Teleo has been called to Guatemala to cure a village of some mysterious fever. He left yesterday. I wish he were here to greet you, but in a month he will return, *no te preocupes.*"

Lucina's heart skipped a beat. Teleo…gone? He wasn't there? That hadn't been part of the master plan! She bit her lip, looking down at the floor, feeling her disappointment mount into her throat.

Lucina, see what happens when you have expectations? You are disappointed after, a voice rang in Lucina's head. *Now you've gone and done it. The man isn't even here.*

"No worries. He will be back. Until then, you can get ready in your new life here," Señora Labotta said, coming back with the iced tea. She stopped when she saw Lucina's face. A light smile played across her lips, she put the tea down, and slowly walked over to where Lucina was seated. Sighing, she sat down next to her guest and patted her knee.

"Señorita, I can see why you might be disappointed," she said. "Patience is the first lesson you must learn in love. People that are impatient will ruin love."

"What does love have to do with this?" Lucina blurted out, perfectly aware that her response was futile. Her cover had been blown probably some time ago: Señora Labotta was not a stupid woman.

"Ah, love has *everything* to do with this," Señora Labotta responded, seriously. "Drink your tea."

*   *   *

Later in the day, Señora Labotta arranged the same tent for her guest in the backyard. Lucina organized her things in the large tent as she had done before, and when all her things were neatly placed, she took out her diary. She hadn't written in it since the last entry two weeks ago.

Dear Diary,   December 27th

I have lost my wits. I have completely gone insane and this diary is proof of this insanity. I am back in Mexico, after having leased my apartment to a homeless woman named Margarita. I am back in my tent, with my few belongings scattered around me, not sure of whether or not I am dreaming this craziness or living it.

Teleo isn't here.

Oh, but I am here now, that's all that matters. I have many things to do. I have to first get a new job (not in computers), then I have to find an apartment, then I have to send for all my things. Of course, I have to find out about work visas and all these things.

One day at a time, right? One day at a time. There's nothing to fear anymore. I will not live in fear anymore. It has done enough damage in my life. It's time for a change.

"Lucina?" called out Señora Labotta from outside the tent. Lucina closed her diary and poked her head out. "Would you like to help me with supper?"

"Certainly, I would love to," Lucina answered, stepping outside. She followed her back to the tiny little dwelling, eager to be in the presence of her favorite woman of all time. As the two women cooked, they talked about Lucina's future plans. Lucina told Señora Labotta that she wished to maybe learn about literature, so Señora Labotta offered her a part-time job at her store, reassuring Lucina that she would perfect her Spanish in no time. Lucina accepted gladly, happy to already have a temporary job.

At least, it's a start, Lucina thought happily.

That evening, they ate on the porch, looking up at the star-lit sky. It was wonderful to be back. Lucina felt peaceful, quiet, and happy. The only thing missing was Teleo, but as Señora Labotta had mentioned, one had to practice patience in love, if indeed Lucina was in love, which she wasn't quite sure.

"How do you know when you are in love?" Lucina questioned Señora Labotta, taking a bite out of the delicious cheese enchilada.

"You know when you are in love when you suddenly feel connected to the whole world, like you are no longer caught in a web, that is love," Señora Labotta replied. "Love is when you are no longer afraid, when you begin to face the many challenges that come at you instead of running away. Love is when you feel like laughing at any little silly thing that happens around you. That is love."

Lucina nodded her head, slowly, thinking her words over.

"Lucina, tell me, have you ever been in love?" the Mexican asked, as she poured herself a glass of red wine.

Lucina sighed, and frowned.

"I don't know really, but I know I have met a lot of bad male shells in my life, some I wish I had never met."

"Do you care to share these stories, I would love to hear them," Señora Labotta said as she offered her guest more red wine. Lucina shrugged, took a long sip of the good Chilean wine, and settled back in her chair.

"Sure, but it might take some time," Lucina replied. "I have so many stories."

"Ah, we have all night. So tell me, who was the first man you fell for?"

Lucina took a deep breath and began her story.

Part Three

Confessions

Chapter 14

It was a cold dark autumn night and I was out wandering the parks of East Montreal with my best friend Stacey. We had decided to venture into a park, when we heard the sound of skateboards hitting the pavement. Being young and adventurous, we walked over to where three adolescents were flipping their skateboards, jumping over cracks in the pavement, and talking loudly. One of them called out to us, so we went towards them and struck up a friendly conversation.

The cutest boy, Charles, eyed me intensely, and after a few minutes, came over and introduced himself. We shook hands, looking at one another shyly. I couldn't help but notice how cute he was. He had short, nicely brushed brown hair, soothing soft brown eyes and pink lips. I was drawn into his aura, and felt what he was feeling.

"Your name is rare," he said, hands in pocket.

"Yes, my mother picked a special name," I replied, conscious of how silly my reply was. I blushed and tried to look indifferent.

His two friends invited us to go to their place and have a beer. I looked nervously over at my best friend, trying to discern if she was feeling anything close to what I was feeling. She looked excited, and nodded her head at the suggestion. The five of us walked over to Charles' friend's house, late in the night, without a care in the world.

Sipping on cold Canadian beers, we settled down to watch television in a dimly lit basement. I don't remember what was playing on the television, I guess my mind was focused elsewhere. When I noticed that Stacey was making out with one of the guys, I began to feel as though maybe this was also my doorway to my first, real kiss.

As Charles came in for the kiss, I closed my eyes and thought that I was in heaven. Such electricity fired between us, such fluidity, that I was certain I had kissed this boy before, maybe in another life, because everything was so perfect.

I was in love from the moment that my lips met his lips.

We saw each other almost every day for three weeks. I had never been happier than those three weeks. It was as though new life were flowing in me, as though I were re-born into the beautiful woman I had always wanted to be. Charles complimented me, bought me things, paid for supper, and made me feel precious. I had never been treated like a queen before.

One weekend, we went to his chalet up North. His father was there as well as his step-mother and they explained to us that we would sleep in separate rooms. Charles and I looked at one another with secretive smiles; of course, I wouldn't be sleeping alone! Or so I thought.

The first night, we made out wildly in my room. When Charles took off my shirt, I froze, and my heart started beating faster. This was not the usual stuff; there was fervor in his movements, almost like he was galloping on a horse and had lost control.

I put my hand on his chest and told him that I wasn't ready for the finale.

"Oh, that's all right," he replied trying to look nonchalant. I smiled and kissed him.

"Do you still love me?" I asked with a laugh.

He looked at me and forced a smile. The next morning, Charles was watching *Highlanders* when I got up. He barely looked at me. When I greeted him with a lazy smile, he kept his eyes glued to the television screen. Sitting down next to him, I felt a cold wind blowing around him. I tried to pretend that nothing odd was happening, but deep inside, I knew something had changed.

The wind had changed directions overnight.

We drove back to the city the following night with his parents and he barely looked over at me during the long car ride home. I felt a deep humiliation, but I didn't understand why, so I sat and stared out the front window, trying to keep the conversation alive with his parents with a fake smile on my lips.

When we got to the metro station, he walked me to the subway doors and kissed me almost distractedly. He seemed in a hurry. I felt a heaviness in my heart.

"I'll call you tomorrow, ok?" he said in a strained voice.

But he didn't call me the next day, nor the day after, nor the day after. I told myself that all was okay, that he was just busy because there had to be a logical reason why my love was not calling me. When I at long last got the phone call, it was November 11th, Remembrance Day of all days.

I picked up the phone and heard his familiar voice.

"Hey, I've been really busy," he said right away.

"Oh, and what were you doing? I waited for your call all week."

"Skateboarding. Listen, Lucina, I've been thinking. I think I don't love you anymore," he said in a faint voice.

I felt my lungs caving in on me. The world all of a sudden seemed dark. There it was, the excuse of a lifetime: He had loved me, but three weeks after, it was over, just like that. I didn't know what to say, so I told him that I didn't understand, that I loved him still.

I began to cry silently, and hanging up the phone, I ran downstairs, out into the cold November night. I ran and cried and ran and cried, and thought that the world was ending around me. For hours I rocked myself on a swing, telling myself over and over again that I would never love again, never love again, never love again.

But of course, things never work out the way we plan them.

*   *   *

Señora Labotta leaned towards Lucina and smiled.

"Things never work out as we plan them, señorita: Life is a game. We need to learn that when we have plans, life can surprise us. The trick in life is to realize nothing is ever constant."

Lucina nodded, her head filled with memories of Charles all of a sudden. She felt as though she were re-living those past feelings of rejection and confusions.

Señora Labotta indicated that she should go on with the next story.

Chapter 15

For half a year, I sank into a bottomless pit of self-pity and depression. I didn't want to go out, and if I did, I would cry at the least thought of Charles. Stacey was there the whole time, trying to cheer me up. It was as though life had become a living hell. I couldn't bear the thought of living without Charles, but then again, he had turned me away, so I had no choice but to try to struggle back into life.

A few months later, while snowboarding alone on a mountain near Montreal, I met another boy. What better way to forget about one guy than with the next one? I thought.

Antoine was a talented filmmaker and snowboarder. The minute that I saw him, I knew that he was trouble, so I kept my distance and tried not to get attached, tried to feign indifference. Yet I was so depressed and lonely that I soon fell for him. Thinking about it today, I feel embarrassed about how desperate I was but we all make mistakes, that much I figured out in love.

He had a charming little smile, a twinkle in his blue eyes, a nice tall thin body. I spent many days with Antoine at his house, looking at snowboarding videos or snowboarding with him. He impressed me with his talent, and slowly, I began to be enthralled by him. Deep inside I knew that what I felt for him was not true love, yet I convinced myself that maybe he was the one for me, since Charles had clearly not been.

The day of my sixteenth birthday, I invited Antoine over to the hall where I was having my party. I had invited many people, most of them acquaintances of my friends. I wanted there to be a huge party for me, wanted to make Antoine believe that I was popular and well-liked. He arrived early, and I paraded him around to all my friends, speaking about his many talents, trying to show him off as though he were my own boyfriend.

Then, I introduced him to Julie.

When Antoine and Julie looked at each other, I felt an electrical current in the air around both of them. I looked at him and tried to catch his attention, and he finally glanced back at me and grinned. Off we were again, through the party hall, walking side by side, just like old times. The incident with Julie had been a hallucination.

During the evening, I drank a lot of beer and lost track of Antoine. It had been my intention to always keep him next to me so that when I would really be drunk, I could topple over on him and accidentally kiss him. That had been my ingenious plan to start going out with him, and I had kept going over the details in my mind all night.

At one point in the night, I wandered over to a dark corner and caught a glimpse of two people making out passionately. Chuckling to myself drunkenly, I thought it would be funny to catch the passionate birds in flight so that I could tease them the next day. I walked near the couple and then my eyes opened wide in horror: Antoine's arms were wrapped around a girl and it wasn't me, it was Julie!

Anger boiling inside of me, I stomped over to where they were making out, and yelled in a loud thunderous voice so that everyone around me could hear, "What the *hell* are you doing?"

They turned to look at me. Julie stared at me with a guilty look.

"Luci, we were just…" Antoine said, a confused look on his face, as if he wanted to say, and what is it to you? He stood back, shoved his hands in his pockets, and stared at me. Slowly, I saw his eyes change. He understood then that I had feelings for him.

Like a young child, I stomped out of the hall into the girl's bathroom, and looked at my pale, contorted face in the mirror. At that moment, I wanted to destroy the bathroom, as well as Antoine and Julie.

*   *   *

Señora Labotta interrupted her guest.

"We often react out of anger when we feel cheated, however sometimes, it is also the ego reacting. Sometimes anger and ego are confused, do you understand, Lucina?"

Lucina reflected a few seconds, biting her lip.

"Perhaps it was my ego, perhaps I felt I had lost a certain game," Lucina said softly.

"The ego sometimes dresses up in anger, and vice versa. The important thing is to realize that it is in our nature to be competitive. Once we realize this, it is easier to lose because we know that there will be many more games to play."

Lucina was silent for a while, and then started speaking once more.

*   *   *

"Luci, I'm so sorry, I didn't know that you…" Julie said slowly as she walked into the bathroom. She looked distraught.

"Yeah, right," I yelled at her, beside myself. "All this time I was telling you that I liked this guy, that I wanted to go out with him, blah blah blah! And what do you do? On my birthday for Christ's sake, you go and make out with him. You are a bitch, and you are no longer my best friend. Fuck off."

Julie stood back, crying. I could see she was upset for real.

"What the hell were you thinking?" I screamed at her.

Locking myself up in a bathroom stall, I slumped down on the seat, silently crying. But I didn't have to yell at Julie; she was crying and I knew that she already regretted what she had done. I walked out of the bathroom and spent the rest of the night ignoring them. In truth, I think it was my ego that was most hurt. I knew that I didn't love Antoine but I had still wanted to conquer him, to feel good about myself again, to retrieve that part of me that Charles had destroyed with those few words over the telephone, I don't love you anymore.

A few days went by, and I spent some time reflecting on my behavior that night. After all, I had told Julie that I was not in love with Antoine, so perhaps it wasn't such a crime in the end, I told to myself. She hadn't stolen him from me: I had never had him in the first place.

Eventually, I picked up the phone and dialed her number. I told her that I forgave her for what had happened and that although it still hurt me inside, if she wanted to go out with Antoine, I would give her my blessing. After calling her, I called Antoine and told him the same thing. I felt relieved. A week later, Julie and Antoine were happily going out. I tried to bury my feelings for him and tried to be happy for both. I reasoned that if I couldn't find love, at least I could try to be happy if others found it. I slowly became friends with Julie again.

After the Antoine-Julie incident, I kept coming back to my story with Charles and the way that he had let me down. It was something that I just couldn't digest and it was something that transformed me into another girl, a mean, manipulating and selfish girl. For about a year, I was a girl of the worst kind; I hung out in bars with Stacey and my quest was to make guys fall for me and soon after, I would simply walk away and never see them again. Darwin was right, I reflected: Survival of the fittest. You either die in the hands of your predator, or you become the predator.

I became the predator and enjoyed my new role.

I met many random boys that year, their names forgotten in the sands of time. One boy here, one boy there, and they were all the same, horny little boys to me. My game was to walk into a party, look for the hottest boy, focus all my attention on him until he had no escape, no possible exit, and then make him come to me. I drew boys to me and then threw them back up like cats throw up hairballs.

They were there to entertain me but never to steal something precious from me again. I could kiss them and the game ended there.

Chapter 16

Like all phases, this one ended abruptly upon the encounter of a stranger in a subway car one hot August afternoon. Stacey and I had been to a rock show that afternoon and we were excitedly talking about the hot singer, when two French guys walked into the metro car and sat down opposite us. Louis didn't catch my eye at first and it took me a few minutes before I noticed that a beautiful golden-eyed boy was giving me furtive glances. When I did notice him, I noted that he was tall, about six feet, wearing blue skater shorts and a Millencollin t-shirt. His hair was short, wavy, bleached-blond and he resembled Richard Gere. He leaned towards us and smiled.

"Hello, my name is Louis, and this is Matt, we're from France," he said in poor English.

I turned and gave Stacey my confident, let-me-handle-these-boys look. I had developed an over-confidence with men, a front that wouldn't ever let me become the prey again. We struck up a conversation on music, and soon enough, I had their phone numbers in hand. Stacey giggled and told me that she had found Louis' friend adorable and that she wanted to definitely see them again. I told her not to worry and that Queen Lucina would cook up something very good.

Little did I know what I was really getting into when I met Louis that afternoon. I had no idea that he would turn my world upside down and throw me off balance completely.

Never underestimate the power of physical attraction.

We saw them the following day, walked around downtown with them, and when they invited us to see a movie, we didn't refuse. I kept staring at Louis and wondering where in the world he had come from. His eyes had such magnetism that I found that I couldn't look anywhere else, and what a gentleman he was at the time, always holding the door for me, always offering to pay drinks for me. Montreal boys were not at all like this lovely charming French man.

The world spun around and around until I completely forgot that I was supposed to be the one running the show. One afternoon, Louis invited me to the movie theatre. I sat myself next to him in the dark, air-conditioned theatre, barely containing my nervousness. As his hand found its way to mine during the movie, the suffering of the last years disappeared and I began to feel the faint flutter of hope in my breast again.

That evening, before parting, he took me aside and told me that he had never felt such electricity before, that he was so happy to have met me. He took my hand and kissed it ever so gently, promising me that he would call the next day.

"Your eyes are like the twinkling stars in the midnight sky," he whispered to me before leaving.

A bell should have gone off at that moment, but I was so relieved to hear such words that I shut off the voice inside me warning me that not everything that glitters is gold.

Louis and I were together almost every day for a month. I thought of nothing else but him and would do nothing else but anticipate the next moment together. Stacey started going out with Matt, so we made a perfect foursome, but Louis and I were living a completely different story, I told myself. Ours was more real than reality, more intense than intensity, more passionate than passion. No words could describe our love, I thought.

He would hold my hand, and I would hold his, and nothing else mattered. Our world was the world itself.

"You know that I am leaving in a few days," he said to me one humid August night. I stopped walking, turning to look up at him. Stillness surrounded us in the lonely streets.

"I don't want to go, not back home. All I have there is a drunk mother, some boring friends, and a shitty job. I want to stay here with you," he sighed. I hugged him passionately and told him that we shouldn't think about such things now, that we should live the moment, live the moment, yet inside I knew that time was catching up to us, and that our love would soon end. How I fought reality that week. I woke up each morning, called him, made plans, ran around all day trying to hold unto him as long as possible. I tried to sleep as little as possible so as to spend as much time as possible in his arms, in his strong, stable arms.

I was almost feverish by the time our last day came around.

The final night together we spent in Mount Royal Park. Louis and I held unto each other, hugging one another ferociously, telling each other that we would write and that I would come the next year, as soon as I had money. All that night we fought time, we fought the urge to fall asleep on the wet ground. Every second mattered.

When he brought me to Berri metro at 7 a.m., I entered a state of shock. I couldn't bear to look at him for fear of bursting into uncontrollable tears. I stared at the metro floor and kept trying to think of mundane things. Taking me in his arms, Louis promised me that he would wait for me. I looked at him and said nothing. I wanted to jump into his arms and say, take me with you! Take me away from here and marry me, and we'll be happy forever and ever! We'll have children, and we'll be the happiest couple on this planet!

The subway bell sounded. He jammed his foot in the closing doors.

"I love you, Luci, don't forget that!" he called, looking at me one last time. The doors closed and I stood gaping at him, my eyes wide in terror.

The love of my life was being taken from me again.

Was that my destiny, to always lose that which I loved?

Chapter 17

Señora Labotta reached for another glass of wine. Her eyes seemed like two bright beams of light when Lucina turned to look at her.

"Your stories fill me with wonder, Luci. They are filled with such innocence and illusions, I am certain you are aware of this, yes?" Señora Labotta said, watching Lucina closely.

Lucina shifted, looking at the floor. *I don't know what to say to this,* she mused.

"Yes, I was quite the romantic I guess," she managed to say. "I didn't live in the real world, that's for sure. I don't regret it now. I see that all girls have to go through this process of disillusionment."

"All *humans,*" Señora Labotta corrected. "All humans have to learn that fairy tales really are just that—tales. But please, go on, continue to speak with the heart."

*   *   *

That year, I obtained my first job working for a French woman in a frippery downtown. She was a horrible, mean boss, but I knew that if I wanted to go to France to see the man of my life, I needed to save up a lot of money. I worked like a dog. The woman was harsh, cold, stern, never thanking me or encouraging me. I grew sick of her perfume at the end of the year.

Louis' letters made me live. I received only a few during the year, but each time the words poured like honey over me, soothing my weeping heart, healing my mind. One day, he wrote telling me that perhaps it would be better if we gave each other freedom during that year, since we couldn't be together. My breath stopped when I read his words and tears formed in my eyes, but I wanted him to be happy, so despite my breaking heart, I wrote back that I agreed. I wrote back telling him that if that was what he wanted, then I didn't mind. Yet of course, I was petrified: What if he met another girl, what if he fell in love with someone else?

His letters became scarcer and scarcer, until finally, I had no news anymore from him. My mind and heart were so set on making my story turn into the most beautiful fairy tale, that I ignored all the warning signs that reality was sending me. Women do that a lot now that I think about it; we pretend that a man is the Prince Charming we have been waiting for. We craft a stranger into Prince Charming, and if he deviates from the picture, we excuse him and keep seeing the Prince instead of the man.

By the end of the year, I had assembled enough money to pay for my vacation to the south of France. I called Louis one afternoon and he sounded surprised to hear from me. I told him happily that in three weeks I could go visit him in the south of France and that I was wondering if I could stay at his house. He answered, somewhat hesitantly, that he would have to ask his mother for permission. What an odd thing to say to me, I thought at the time. As before though, I pushed my doubts away and waited patiently for his answer.

A few seconds later, he took the phone again and said that it would be no problem. I hung up feeling as though the sun were shining again for the first time since the previous summer. I was going to go meet the future man of my children, the man with the glittering golden eyes, the man who would be faithful to me and only me! He would stand by my side, would cook meals for me, and we would have a house by the sea.

The three weeks prior to my departure were the longest three weeks of my life. I kept looking at his picture, thinking how wonderful it would be to be kissing those soft lips again. I imagined how he would be waiting for me at the train station, roses in hand, a light breeze whisking through his hair, a faint smile across his thick lips.

One sunny May day, I settled my seventeen year old body into Air France's cushioned seats and smiled dreamily to myself as the plane took off. This is it! I kept thinking to myself. I am about to meet my future husband. Just like in the movies, but better.

At the airport of Marseilles, I took a train to Louis' hometown. In the train, I was so nervous that I couldn't eat a thing. I kept getting up and pacing up and down the aisle, pretending I was feeling sick to my stomach. In reality, I was starting to imagine that maybe he would not be at the train station to meet me, or maybe he would send one of his friends instead, or maybe his house was filled with porn stars.

That afternoon, I arrived in the middle of nowhere. A single wooden platform greeted me, as well as a deserted train station. A few trees lined the small, run-down train station, and the only sound that could be heard was the sound of little birds chirping somewhere in the empty village. No one else got off the train at my station. When the train puffed away, I was invaded with an intense feeling of fear in my stomach.

What if it's all in my head after all? I suddenly thought. What if there's no way this is going to work?

Out of the shadows of the silent train station emerged Louis. His hair was brown now, but he was still wearing a skater t-shirt and the same Vans shoes. He smiled awkwardly, scrutinizing me from head to toe. I felt myself turn red. We stared at one another, and skipped the greeting part. I walked silently by his side and could tell that he was searching for his words. Was he disappointed? Was he happy? Was he nervous? I could tell nothing from his

poker face, nothing at all, and that was scarier than anything else
I had known before.

"How have you been?" he asked me as we walked towards
God knew where.

"Okay, I worked a lot this year to see you and I'm happy to be
here," I replied cautiously, observing his reaction.

He nodded his head, looking straight ahead, his face blank.

Louis' house was nestled in the heart of the French village,
surrounded by beautiful exotic plants and trees. In the back was
a parrot named Coco, and two scratched-up cats. In a dramatic
fashion, his mother greeted me, brought beers and made me sit
down at a small wooden table. I could smell the alcohol on her
breath right away. Louis looked embarrassed.

What have I done? I thought to myself.

Supper was a strained event. Everyone seemed uncomfortable and his mother tried to make the atmosphere more comfortable by chattering about mundane things. She kept repeating
how delightful it was to have a Canadian eat at their table. After
our meal, Louis led me to my bedroom upstairs. The room was
small, but comfortable and cozy. Glancing towards Louis' room, I
felt a wave of nervousness float through my body. I unpacked and
a few minutes later, a man's voice echoed in the house. Curious,
I went downstairs and met his best friend, Richard, who was five
feet tall, had short, wavy black hair and intense brown eyes. He
had a very scrawny little body, which reminded me almost of a
puppet's body, and was swinging his skinny legs on the kitchen
chair. When he saw me, he gave me a big grin.

At least he seems happy to see me, I thought miserably. At
least he smiles and seems like he wants to talk to me.

The first night in the south of France was terrifying. I felt
completely disoriented and frightened, but I tried to reassure
myself. I slept poorly that night. The following day, Louis introduced me to his other friend, Paul, and the four of us headed to

a village fiesta. We sat down at a picnic table in the middle of the
town party. I sat next to Louis, awkwardly trying to find something to chat about, but he seemed distracted, disinterested even.
We ordered cold beers.

Instead of talking to me, Louis wandered over to the bar and
started talking to two hot older, well-shaped women. At first, I
made myself believe that he knew them from school and that
they were discussing homework. I made up a story that the beautiful thin big-breasted blond was having trouble with her gram-
mar and that Louis was explaining to her some basic rules. But
after an hour, I started to realize that things were not going to
work out the way I had dreamed: This man was clearly not my
Prince Charming.

I felt a familiar stab in my heart.

*   *   *

"Did you know," Señora Labotta interrupted, "that the stab in the
heart is actually real? The heart is the most sensitive organ of the
whole body, and it is what I call the Truth Detector. When we
feel a stab in the heart, it is because we are feeling a lie and our
heart detects it right away, before the mind does."

Lucina was surprised to hear this.

"Tell me more, Señora Labotta."

"The heart is the true connection between the earth and the
heavens. When we live something unjust, it is usually the heart
that suffers first. If we happen to have a strong heart, then the
pain loges usually somewhere in another organ which is weaker
than the rest, be it the liver, the stomach, the brain, and so forth."

"Really? That is interesting," Lucina said, thoughtful.

"I apologize for all my interruptions. Please continue," the
Mexican said, as she settled back into the couch.

*   *   *

Richard noticed my deep anxiety and bought me a few drinks throughout the night. In a fit of emotion that I could no longer conceal, I turned to him and explained to him that I had come to France to see Louis because we had once been in love, or so I thought. I told him that I wasn't sure of anything anymore and asked him if he thought I was a stupid girl. Richard shook his head and cleared his voice.

"Everything changes, nothing stays the same," he answered in a quiet voice. "You know, Heraclitus used to say this; 'You can never step twice in the same river for fresh waters are ever flow-ing'. I learnt that when my girlfriend left me for another guy, a friend of mine."

I remained silent. Louis had bought the two girls drinks, and they were comfortably leaning against the bar, laughing. I felt my throat contract.

"Yeah, I guess you're right. I had so many hopes, you know," I replied, my throat clenching up and the tears rising to my eyes.

"Luci, if you don't mind me saying so; you're a smart girl, but maybe you see things that are not really there? I mean, Louis was a different guy on vacation. Here, this is the real Louis, and sometimes, I know him, he can be a real jerk."

I closed my eyes momentarily, feeling nauseous again.

"How can a person ever really know anyone? I mean, the man you fell in love with was only a part of the man you are see-ing now," Richard continued. "Louis is a flirt, and unfortunately, you have to witness this tonight. I'm sorry. If ever you feel like hanging out with me, you're welcome."

The rest of the evening I spent next to Richard, and got so drunk that when Louis eventually sauntered back, I simply ig-nored him. He got my message, as I had gotten his. The drive back home was silent and tense. Richard did his best to loosen things up by playing some punk music extremely loud and driv-ing at 180 km per hour on narrow country roads.

I couldn't care less if we crashed that night. My dream had been shattered and I felt like my whole life was a joke

When we returned to Louis' house, Richard hugged me and told me that whenever I wanted to hang out with him, he would be more than happy to show me around the town. He added that if I needed a sympathetic ear, that I could count on him. I was comforted by his words, but as Louis unlocked the front door, I felt a pang of fear. What was I going to do for two weeks? There I was, stuck with strangers, realizing that I had been a naïve little girl living in her head. I had no friends, no family around me, and my only comfort was the presence of a tiny guy who reminded me of a miniature doll.

I went up to my new room, avoiding Louis' eyes. He went immediately to the bathroom, took a shower, and then walked out, fully dressed. I waited for him to close his door, and then I followed his example. I am such an idiot, I kept thinking as the water massaged my tired skin. I am such an idiot. There are no dumber girls on this planet than me right now. Who in their right mind treks to another country, only to realize that the Prince is a myth?

Louis and I lived together in the same place for two weeks, almost in complete isolation one from the other. I spent my days with Richard, and Louis spent his days with his other friends. I did my best to hurry past his bedroom at night, jump in the shower, brush my teeth, and close my door. In the morning, we would exchange a little morning talk and then respectively head out to our individual plans.

All would have been fine, had I not decided to give in to Richard's advances. Before I knew it, one night after getting wasted, I kissed him. From then on, I simply pretended that I was attracted to him, that I wanted to live something with him. I felt so abandoned that I turned to the first man that showed me signs of kindness. I still hadn't learnt that in times of chaos, turn to yourself for stability.

Louis reacted to the news that Richard and I were going out the same way he reacted to everything else: He pretended that he didn't give a damn.

There came a night, near the end of the holiday, when I got plastered again at another village party. It had become a habit of mine to get really drunk in order to erase reality. I felt so humiliated and rejected that alcohol was my only comfort at that time. Paul and Richard had to carry me to their car, and at Louis' house, they left me literally in his arms.

"What do I do now?" I heard Louis grumble to his friends. His friends shrugged and told him to put me to bed and to be a good boy.

Gingerly, as though carrying a wounded person, he carried me upstairs and lay me down on my bed. I was extremely drunk, and remember thinking, here is my chance, maybe he will finally admit to me that he still loves me. Ah, how stupid I was then.

Without being conscious of what I was doing, I took off my shirt, teetered around the room and fell down on my bed, staring at him. Louis was rooted in the doorway, looking as though he had seen a ghost. His face unexpectedly softened, he took a step, then two, and ended sitting down on the bed not far from me.

The room was spinning.

"How are you feeling, Luci?" he asked me.

"Pretty messed up, thank you," I answered, giggling for no reason. My mind was gone.

"And what…what do you want to do now?"

Staring up at him, I pulled him down on me. Without any remorse, he kissed me and held me. I was drunk but not drunk enough to lose my virginity that night. Somewhere, my mind must have still been working.

When the full impact of the previous night hit me the next morning, I felt giddy and disoriented. How could something like that happen to me? He had treated me like crap, and I had repaid him by making out with him? I was so disgusted with myself that I vomited in the bathroom. That day, I lay in bed and felt like the tiniest bug on the planet. Where is your self-respect, a voice whispered. Where is your self-respect?

But my heart had tasted hope and a young girl so easily jumps on hope. I struggled out of bed, thinking that I would go see Louis and at last have a heart-to-heart with him.

"What happened last night..." I began softly, seeing him in the kitchen.

"Was an accident," he finished, getting up quickly from the table without looking at me. He washed his dishes calmly and left the house. I stood there speechless and completely heart-broken. I slouched down in the hard kitchen chair, feeling the tears coming to my eyes.

The last few days, we tried to ignore each other. I felt sadness in the air, sadness that things had turned out the way they had, sadness that perhaps our time together could have been spent differently. I felt Louis observing me at a distance, as though he wanted to say something to me but never got around to saying it.

When Louis and Richard drove me to the airport on the last day, I felt Louis' eyes on me the whole time, as though he were deliberating what could have been. In the heavy silence that reigned in the car, it was as though I discerned his deep desire to go back to last year, to the way he had been in Montreal, to that part of him which maybe had been more real and authentic.

At the airport, he hugged me good-bye and held me tightly in his arms as though he were afraid to never see me again. I closed my eyes and felt my heart skip a beat. It was in his embrace that I at last understood what had happened between us in France; he had been too afraid to surrender, too afraid to jump into the unknown with me. The mountain ahead had been too menacing, too big for him.

It was easier to flirt with strangers than dive into his soul.

Smiling awkwardly, I told him to take care of himself. His eyes followed me all the way through customs and when I turned around, it was not Richard who had misty eyes but Louis.

I never saw him again.

Chapter 18

I realized as I was coming back to Canada that some stories simply cannot evolve; they are fragments in time, they simply start but never end. Like a photograph, they are there to remind you that something was once in your life and no longer is.

I cried so much when I got back home. My dream had been shattered. The man I thought I was going to marry had not wanted to give me the time of day. He had walked into my life, brought love to my heart, and then, had vanished. I felt betrayed again, but this time by God.

*　　*　　*

"Ah yes, blaming God for everything," Señora Labotta sighed, stretching. "That is typical of humans. Whenever something bad happens to them, it is God's fault. But whenever something good happens, it is now their doing. Tell me señorita, do you believe in God?"

Lucina took a sip of the wine and frowned.

"I do believe in something being greater than me, but what, I don't know."

Señora Labotta nodded.

"Perhaps God is something that can never be grasped by humans. But no matter, we should not be talking about God when obviously at this moment you are cursing the powers that be."

*　　*　　*

Indeed, I cursed God from the depths of my soul, shook my fists at the greater powers, and told them that I just couldn't take the pain and the suffering anymore. My heart had been shot down so many times, that I wanted to pull myself away from suffering forever. I resigned myself to never loving again after Louis. I fervently prayed and prayed so that I would be strong enough to spend my life alone forever, with cats, some friends and peace. It was then that I decided to study computers because they would never betray me, they would depend on me, and I would fix them. They would not stab my heart, they would not step on me; they would hum and I would he happy.

For two long years, I maintained my solitary life. I went out with friends and when I went out, I would keep a safe distance from guys and talk my way around them, reminding myself that all they wanted was sex. Every gesture became an attack on my heart, and the only thing normal to do was build many walls around my heart.

No one would penetrate there ever again, I promised myself.

One night, my friends invited me to go camping north of Montreal and a charming guy came with us. I knew Marc from before; he was a cute skater guy with large brown hazel eyes, short, brown hair, and a confident stride, all attractive features.

The little voice in my head said, what are you doing? Another man will cause you only grief and suffering, but I managed to push the voice out of my head and told it that I was in control for real. I am not going to fall in love this time, I promised myself. Not over my dead body,

That night, Jason, Miriam, Marc and I made a campfire and drank some beer. I started to feel passion invading my senses, and looking over at Marc, I imagined what it would be like to kiss his attractive lips. He seemed lost in his own thoughts, oblivious to me.

When Jason and Miriam retreated to their lover's nest, I glanced over at Marc. He was picking dirt off his shoes and I had to clear my throat a few times to get his attention. He lifted his intense eyes on me, smiling. The fire cast a haunting shadow across his face.

"So, I guess it's good night then," he said, stretching. I nodded my head.

"I don't feel comfortable sleeping alone in my tent," I said to him, taking a deep breath. He looked up in surprise. I was surprised myself by my own boldness.

"I have a pretty big bed in there," he said, pointing to a large red four person tent a few feet away. "It's a queen size blow-up mattress. I only sleep on the best."

We stared at each other. He got up and led the way back to his tent. Once inside, I glanced at the blown-up queen-sized bed and was relieved to see it was indeed big enough to have a lot of space between us, in case I changed my mind, but I knew I wasn't going to change my mind. He lay down on the bed, crossing his arms under his head, observing me silently. His stillness made me uneasy. I gulped down a large ball which had mysteriously moved up in my throat.

Why now? I was asking myself.

Why not? answered a voice. What's the point in waiting when you know damn well there isn't one good man out there worth your virginity? You might as well get rid of it now, so that it never bothers you again. Might as well just do it, like that Nike slogan says everywhere.

Just do it.

Just do it.

Just do it.

"Do you feel like giving me a massage?" Marc's voice cut into my thoughts. My heart started pounding. I said that it would be my pleasure, he turned over, and I began to massage him gently. I felt the strength of his firm muscles under my fingers and found myself becoming exhilarated.

This is not love, I repeated to myself over and over again. This is sex. Only sex.

He seemed to be drifting off to sleep, when abruptly, he opened his eyes and flipped over on his back. I remained sitting on top of him, looking down at him, my hands on his shoulders. When his strong arms pulled me down on him, I knew that this would be my first time.

Undressing me with the speed of light, he threw my clothes over his shoulder like an expert in the field. I lay on my back, waiting with eyes shut tight for that gigantic pain that was supposed to cut my body in two. After a few minutes of nothing tremendously painful happening, I tapped him lightly on the shoulder and asked him innocently what was going on.

He chuckled.

"What do you mean?"

"I mean, I'm not feeling any pain, you know…"

There was silence. He propped himself up and stared at me.

"Well, maybe you're not a virgin after all!" he said with a laugh. I didn't laugh back.

The whole scene lasted about ten minutes and when he was done, he slipped quickly back into his boxers, threw the condom out the tent, and lay back down on the bed. I slipped quietly under the covers and closed my eyes. We didn't say a word for some time and then I admitted that it wasn't what I had expected. Marc didn't say a word. He turned over on his side and soon after, was fast asleep.

The next morning, he acted as though nothing out of the ordinary had happened. When I asked him how he felt towards me, he shrugged and said that he wasn't a couple guy anyway, that he wanted to be free in life. I felt a stab but concluded silently to myself that it was better that way. No strings attached, no pain, no love, no hell. It was all good.

All good.

When we returned from our camping trip, Marc asked for my phone number, and a few nights later I received a phone call from him. He invited me over to his house to play a game of chess, I agreed to come over, and the very same thing happened again, except this time, it lasted five minutes instead of ten.

Looking up at the ceiling, I said to myself, hell, if this is what sex is, then I am glad that I did not to waste my life waiting for it. Marc didn't seem to notice that my mind was wandering.

Our five-minute marathon took place once in a while after that. I was always left hoping that maybe the next time, I might feel a vague pleasurable feeling, but pleasure never came. One day, I simply sat up and spoke to him bluntly.

"Listen, Marc, I don't know about you, but this is rather bland and empty, I think I want to wait for something better."

He looked away and shrugged.

"What you seek you will never find. Love is for little girls and their fairy tales. Welcome to the real world. Here, you try to be happy with what you find. Sex is good, you should try to enjoy it."

I remained silent and stared out the grey window. After a few minutes of contemplation, I turned and looked at him.

"You know, I still believe in love and what we have is called fucking. I am not an animal; I want something more out of life, so this is the end."

He didn't argue with me.

Chapter 19

A gust of wind blew through the slightly opened window in the living room and tussled Señora Labotta's long hair. As Señora Labotta's hair floated around her, Lucina was once more reminded of witches.

"Ah, the sacrifice of the virgin!" the Mexican said, shaking her head. "How many women act like that I do not know, but it is so terribly sad to see how we surrender to whatever crosses our path. I figure you now realize that surrendering to men just out of boredom is a poor thing to do to your spirit, yes?"

Lucina shifted on the couch and looked down at her hands.

"Yes, I guess that I just didn't care anymore. I stopped believing I was worth something special. After all those bad experiences, I just didn't care who was going to be my first. I would do things differently now..."

* * *

I know that I did the right thing telling Marc that I wanted something more out of life, something more than what some called "the old in-and-out". Now that I was no longer seeing him, I turned my attention back to cegep and back to the computers I loved so much.

During my time in cegep, I started to go to underground raves in Montreal. I never did drugs, but I did indulge in dancing all night to the sound of trance, goa and drum'n'bass. The music would take me to another world, a world in which no pain, no suffering, no loneliness existed. In that world I was fluid, free, and could be whatever I wanted to be.

For several months, I drifted in and out of raves, like a ghost. I preferred to be invisible in order to keep people away. Dancing was my balm, my own personal healing medicine, and I wanted to dance and sweat all the past away, to forget about those guys who had broken my heart, who had made me feel little.

One night, as I was dancing by myself in a corner, a man came up to me and smiled.

"What's your name?" he called out over the music.

"Luci, and yours?"

"Brian."

I stopped dancing, wiped the sweat from my forehead, and walked over with him to the chill-out room where the music was less loud. He plopped himself down on the purple couch and smiled. The dark light made it hard for me to see him, but I could tell he was fit, taller than I, had blond, very short hair and bright blue eyes. Although not the most beautiful man I had seen, he had a spark in him that caught my eye.

"So, what do you do in life, Brian?" I asked him, looking into his baby blue shining eyes.

"I'm a psychology student at McGill University."

Ah ha! I thought with pleasure, an intelligent man who studies psychology so he must be a good guy, right? My heart skipped a beat.

We talked all night about life and Brian admitted to me that he enjoyed reading philosophy, travelling, dancing and writing poetry. By the end of the evening, my head was spinning with hope. He might be the one, I thought to myself, watching his twinkling eyes. He might be the one. There is still hope.

Brian took my phone number and the next morning, I received a phone call from him asking me whether I would be interested in going for a beer that very same night at Baloo's. It took me a split second before I answered that I would love to. We met and picked out a nice, quiet table near the window of the crowded bar. He ordered some beers and we started drinking together, warmly smiling at one another. During the evening, I kept noticing how I felt dizzy and disoriented around him. I thought that maybe it was the beer affecting me, but in reality, I think it might have been something much more complicated than that.

"I've never felt this way about anyone in my life," Brian declared a few hours later. He turned to look at me. "It's like I'm in a vortex and my head is spinning."

My mouth dropped open. I too felt like a vortex was surrounding me, but hadn't wanted to tell him my thoughts, scared that he might laugh at me.

"Luci, I can't help but admit that ever since I met you the other night, I felt like I knew you from before, like we had lived other lives together. When I stare at you, I feel I understand your soul and you understand mine. I hope you don't think I am crazy!" he said, with a smile perched on his lips.

The little voice crept up at that moment. Luci, he's got you on his hook, the voice whispered. He's just another fake one, run away and don't look back. This one is a master of words, master of philosophy, he's cunning and wise and crafty. But once more, I ignored the voice and resumed my intense evening.

It takes time before we realize that our intuition is a powerful tool of protection.

At around midnight, we walked out of the smoky bar together and stood in the nearly deserted avenue. Brian sighed dramatically, looking intensely at me.

"I would invite you over but that would surely ruin the magic," he said slowly. "I don't want to rush whatever this is. You are such a nice girl, Luci."

He leaned in and hugged me.

I hugged him back, a bit disappointed, and walked away

shakily. He called after me that he would love to see me again soon, and I turned around and smiled, filled with confusion.

What was that all about? I was wondering as I took the metro home. Does a guy hug a girl he feels so strongly about? I shook my head and tried to focus on something else. The voice came back, stronger this time. That man is a fraud! warned the voice. That man is going to hurt you, like all the others. I angrily pushed the voice out of my head, forbidding it to come close to me again.

The same week, Brian and I went walking around downtown and again, I couldn't shake the vortex pulling me towards him. It was as though a part of me was merging with him, was almost being sucked by him. Something was beginning to break inside of me, and I desperately had to ask Brian what he felt for me in order to avoid the crash. One afternoon, I spoke to Brain as we sat in a crowded Burger King on Saint Catherine Street. Nervously, I took a huge sip of my soda, turned to face him, and finally blurted out that I wanted to know what he really felt for me.

"To tell you the truth Luci, I'm not looking for a relationship right now, it has nothing to do with you," he said slowly, avoiding my eyes. "It's just...I want to remain open to life, you understand?"

I looked at him in confusion. What had all those nice words the other night meant, was he messing with my mind?

"I don't understand, you were saying that you felt something special for me," I fumbled, my face turning red with embarrassment.

"Yes and I do, it's just we don't know each other enough. I don't want to ruin anything by being hasty, you know what I mean?" Brian squeezed my hand and took a long sip of his soda while I shook my head and looked out the window into the busy street scene in front of us.

At that time, I pretended that his words made total sense. I nodded and told Brian that indeed, we didn't know each other enough to start anything, but something was off. Something was strange about that man, yet I consoled myself by saying that maybe I was just afraid, afraid to let go and let life carry me to a new place.

During the first year, Brian and I spent a lot of time together. I craved him like a heroin addict craves the needle. We began a religious ceremony of hugs each time we were together; he would walk towards me slowly, majestically wrap his arms around me, and I would close my eyes, rocking in his arms like a child. We would spend evenings hugging, on a couch, in a park, in a bar, in a restaurant. Hugs became life for me.

The hugs, though, one day became torture. I only wanted to kiss him, be held by him in a more physical way, be filled by him, but Brian only wanted to hug, and so I cast my eyes to the skies and prayed that he would find his way to my lips eventually, and maybe to something more promising.

The inevitable truth came one day as we were lying down on his bed. He looked at me and cleared his throat.

"I would love for you to meet this girl I'm dating, she's really sweet and you guys would really get along."

My chest convulsed as though I had been electrocuted. I turned and looked at him, blinked rapidly, and asked him to repeat what he had just said. He repeated it, looking me straight in the eye and smiling.

"Oh," was all I could think of saying. "I get it."

The last months of my life flashed before my eyes. It had all been a joke, I realized then, my eyes opening for the first time. His words, his hugs, his praises, it had all been a delusion. He had never wanted me; he had only wanted affection and hadn't cared whether he led me down a dead-end path. I glared at Brian, made up a lame excuse about having something to do at home, and took the metro that night feeling completely disoriented and dejected. After hearing him tell me that we could no longer hug because it might be inappropriate considering he was now seeing someone, I felt I had no more energy.

I felt drained, miserable and tired.

I saw Brian less, but when I did, he still showed me the same affection as before. He would still tell me beautiful things, and make sure that I knew I was his "girl, best friend and advisor". I couldn't shake myself from him. I would wait for his phone call, and then when he would call, I would cancel all my previous plans and head straight for him with hope in my heart.

*   *   *

"Women have to learn that their hearts speak the truth," Señora Labotta piped in, staring hard at Lucina. "Women have such a powerful intuition when it comes to the outside world, but very little do they trust their intuitions. They usually choose to close their eyes because they know reality might be less beautiful than they expect it to be."

"I agree," Lucina said, shaking her head, remembering how blind she had been. "I did hear my heart and the little voice talking to me. It had warned me that Brian was not for me, but I was masochistic."

Señora Labotta stood up, went to the window, and pulled the drapes back to let the moon shine into the living room. The clock on the table read 1:32 a.m. Lucina stifled a yawn.

"Shall we call it a night?" Lucina ventured. Señora Labotta spun around, looking shocked.

"Not at all, I want to hear the end of these addictions of yours, let us hear the rest."

*   *   *

This addiction lasted three whole years. During that period, I kept hoping that Brian would wake up and realize that I was his love, the woman who would stand by him, love him throughout old age, take care of him if he fell sick. I would be there every single moment of his life. Each time we would see each other, I would pretend that the old feelings of love for him had changed to friendship but in reality, I kept falling more and more for him.

Brian was the man, and no one could prove otherwise.

Of course, in such obsessive cases as this one, something had to come along and burst my bubble. Something did come along. In December, two and a half years after my first meeting with Brian, he called me and invited me to his house for a week-end. His parents lived in the state of New York and since I had never actually been there, I decided that it might be exciting to discover a new place and see the man who kept my heart beating every day.

And maybe, just maybe, this would be the chance I had been waiting for all this time.

I packed a light bag, said good-bye to Stacey, and jumped on the Greyhound bus heading towards the States. On the bus, I listened to Jewel and sang along with her;

"These foolish games, are tearing me apart, and your thoughtless words, are breaking my heart, you're breaking my heart."

When I got to the bus terminal, Brian greeted me in his usual manner: A big, long, dramatic hug. I was so happy to see him that I blabbered incoherent gibberish all the way to his home. His house was of modest appearance and his parents seemed like the typical parents; friendly, welcoming and sociable. Energetically, he escorted me upstairs to his brother's bedroom, told me that I could settle myself in and make my little nest.

"I'm so glad we're finally going to spend a few days together, my dear!" he said charmingly, hugging me with vigor.

That very same night he had a party and invited a few people over. I was somewhat disappointed that we would not be spending some quality solo time, but I figured that if that was the way he wanted things, then it was the best way to proceed. Brian's friends arrived around 8 p.m., brought their drinks, and we seated ourselves comfortably in the living room, popping open our beers in unison. I noticed two attractive-looking girls seated not far from Brian but thought nothing of it, telling myself they were just friends.

It took me some time to realize, later on in the evening, that Brian was missing. I looked around downstairs for him, and when I didn't see him anywhere, ventured silently upstairs. When I reached the top of the stairs, I was horrified to see two pairs of legs intertwined on his bed. I could only see the legs sticking out since the rest was hidden, but it was enough to see that one pair belonged to Brian and another pair belonged to a mysterious girl.

A familiar feeling of pain shot into my stomach and I closed my eyes to stop from falling down the stairs. He had brought me there to show me that? To hurt me again? It was going to be re-run of the France catastrophe, I thought with horror. I held unto the banister and pretended that I had not seen anything at all, that it was all in my head, all in my head. I turned on my heel and ran down the stairs, colliding into one of his friends who had a beer in hand and a grin on his face.

"Hey there, *bella chica.*"

I smiled meekly at Steven. I was stuck there for four days. What to do, I pondered. Suffer endlessly or hurt him back with his best friend? I looked at Steven and then thought better of it. Luci, you've been there and done that already, remember Richard? What did that bring you? Nothing but emptiness, so leave it alone, the voice whispered from within.

I spent the evening talking with Steven and when Brian decided to grace us with his godly presence, he did so with a big grin. Go fuck yourself, I was thinking, as I continued playing chess with his best friend. You little shit.

When everyone left his house at around midnight, Brian

yawned and wished me a good night. I muttered, "The same to
you" and closed my door. By then, I was plastered. I had drunk
so much alcohol to forget the scene that I had drunk myself into
near unconsciousness. I hit my bed and was about to pass out
when a timid knock was heard at my door. I shook my head, realizing where I was.

"Yes, who's there?" I mumbled, opening my eyes. The room
spun around me.

'It's me, Brian. Can I come in? I have trouble sleeping," a
little voice said.

A bell should have gone off in my head at that point. The
light bulb should have flashed on and the tiny voice should have
yelled, Luci, tell him to go to hell, tell him to leave you alone, and
get out of here. But instead, I blinked back my stupor and felt a
rush of hope flowing through my veins. What if he declares his
undying love to me tonight? What if he admits that all this time
he was wrong, that he is sorry for not having seen clearer? What
if now, at long last, he will cradle me and say that he doesn't need
anyone else but me in his life?

All girls learn from their blindness sooner or later.

A few seconds went by before I replied that he could come
in. He confidently walked in, closed the door behind him, and
sauntered over to where I was lying, out of my body nearly.

"Oh, Luci, you are the only woman who understands me, you
know that?"

At long last, here it was. The epiphany was happening and he
would be mine forever. I tried to shake myself into consciousness.

"Luci, you have understood me like no other being on this
earth, and I am so grateful for having you in my life."

There were the magic words.

"You are so beautiful, so perfect. I wish…I wish that I could
make love to you."

I stopped breathing and the world spun even faster.

"It has been so long that I wanted to sleep with you, but I just held back, held back because I didn't want to ruin our deep, spiritual relationship. But now, I think that we're ready to move on."

He turned towards me, his breath smelling of strong liquor, I turned towards him, my eyes barely able to contain my exhilaration. While he kissed me and started to take my clothes off, I looked at him in the dark and tried to catch his eyes, but he kept looking above my head. We started to have sex, but then I realized something wasn't quite normal: It was as though he wasn't able to get it up.

I started worrying that it was my fault or that it was that I was inexperienced. The truth was that he was just too drunk. When he finally did succeed, I almost didn't feel a thing and then it was over. I lay next to him in dead silence. Brian abruptly spoke.

"Luci, if I could love anyone in the world it would be you. But the truth is, I can never love anyone. I'm too messed up, you know. I would try anything on this planet just for the heck of it. For example, if Satan would knock on my door tomorrow and ask to come in my body, I would welcome him. Why not? Everything here is worth trying. So what I mean is that, I would love you if I could, but I can't. Love just ain't for me, you know?"

At the sound of his words, my drunkenness magically wore off, and my eyes began to fill with tears. I stared up at the ceiling and closed my eyes shut, pretending that I hadn't heard his words, pretending that it hadn't been him talking to me.

"Please, don't be hurt, I want to be honest with you, Luci," he said in the darkness.

"You're being honest with me?" I spat out angrily. "You had to figure this out, *after* you slept with me? Was that the thing? You just wanted to sleep with me and now you're done, bye bye Luci?"

I was fuming. I grabbed my clothes and got dressed in a hurry, my heart doing flips in my chest. Brian remained silent for a minute or two.

"I do love you, Luci, it's just that I destroy everything I touch, I have this knack for it, you know. I'm messed up and don't want to mess you up."

"It's already too late!" I snapped at him, standing up.

Brian got up, looking peevish in the shadows of the tiny room. I wanted to kick him out of the room. He fumbled around a bit, the door opened and closed, and I was left alone.

"My God, what have I done to deserve this?" I said out loud, tears falling down my face.   The universe didn't answer. If it had answered, it would have probably said to me that it was all my doing, that I should stop living in fairy tales, and keep my feet firmly on the ground.

Chapter 20

"The hardest thing," Señora Labotta said with a sigh, "Is indeed keeping your two feet on the ground when you fall in love. Passion makes the brain muddled, and when our brains no longer function, our feet are no longer on the ground. I think everyone has felt this way before, Lucina."

"Yes, but the hard part is deciphering when the brain is muddled and when it is not," Lucina replied, staring out the window again. "I mean, when we love, it seems that nothing is as it used to be. Whether we are blind or connected to the universe is so hard to tell. For me, I never knew if I was losing my mind or gaining it."

Señora Labotta nodded her head sympathetically. A few seconds of silence passed.

"True love is like gaining super powers," the Mexican responded. "These powers though, for some people, are too intense and they end up using them wrongly or simply ignoring them altogether. I understand your dilemma, believe me. What is real is hard to tell, but a good indicator of true love is the way your heart feels, the way you feel around that person. Love has many facets, and through time we become wiser and learn which facet we do not need to live anymore."

Lucina nodded and resumed where she had left off.

* * *

When I returned home after the week-end in New York, the first thing I did was go to the river near my house and I threw everything Brian had ever given me into the water; a shirt he had made me, a statue he had bought me, and a few more random things. I watched them sail down the river and yelled at the top of my lungs that I wanted him out of my life forever.

I spent many weeks trying to forget him, and when he called, I didn't return his calls, or if I did, I would be snappy with him on the phone. I felt so lonely at times that I just ached to call him, ached to forgive him for his cold nature, but things had turned so sour that forgiveness was not an option anymore. I labored each day to erase his memory from my mind and heart and the task was painful and long.

One October night, I had a horrific nightmare.

I dreamed that I was in my bed and that at the foot of my bed was a white man in a hooded brown cloak. The hood went down over half his pale face and he was chanting some weird words in a language I didn't understand. In my dream, the man was trying to take my spirit from me. I felt that he was pulling on my invisible spirit and trying to suck it up, and I fought him, it seemed, all through the night. When morning came, I awoke in a fright and realized that I was drenched in sweat. Looking around my room, I remembered the terrible nightmare as though it had actually taken place.

Every night for the following three weeks I had the same frightening dream. Each time, the man would appear at the foot of my bed, would be wearing the brown cloak and half his face would be hidden. Once I tried to yell at him to go away but no words came out of me. It was an endless battle against something I didn't understand.

"Luci, I'm so worried about you," my mother sighed as she saw my pale, white face one morning. "Can you tell me what's wrong with you?"

"Mom, just having weird nightmares, nothing to worry about," I replied, not looking her in the eyes. I didn't want to worry her, knowing her paranoid nature.

One day, a friend of mine phoned me and said something peculiar. He explained to me that he had been having dreams about me, and in these dreams he had been seeing a hooded man following me around my apartment. I could not believe my ears, so I questioned him further, but he could tell me nothing more. I decided to invite him over one night, just to see if I could find out other clues as to what could possibly be wrong with me.

When John came over, he sat down on my couch, turning a worried face towards me.

"There is definitely something not normal going on in here," he mumbled distractedly. I asked him how he could possibly know these things. He shrugged and explained that in his family, people had special gifts, such as feeling unnatural phenomena. I was skeptical but didn't want to offend him; I had never really believed in ghosts before.

"It seems to me that it's coming from your bedroom," he muttered, as he carefully walked over to my bedroom. For a moment, he closed his eyes and then reopened them. "He's in here right now, whoever he is, and he does not like this one bit."

"What the hell do you mean?" I sputtered out.

"The hooded man, he's here observing us and he doesn't like me."

John walked over to my bed and faced me suddenly.

"Luci, have you opened some sort of door to the other realm lately?" he demanded. I was completely baffled and could not even respond for a few moments. I shook my head, showing him that I had no clue what he was talking about.

"Look John, I mean, I study computers and don't really believe all this hocus-pocus stuff, that's from the movies," I began. His serious look stopped me.

"Luci, either you can be serious about this or not. I am here to help you, and if you want my help, I'll give it to you. Now, do you want to get rid of this presence or not?" he said emphatically.

"Yeah, I do, but I don't know what to do!" I cried out, feeling desperate and lost.

John told me that we would call the spirit forth and tell him to leave me in peace. I drew myself together and thought, might as well play along, what if this thing works? We sat facing one another and John asked me to bring out a white candle. Then, he lit the candle, and in a deep voice explained to me that he would communicate with the spirit.

"If at any moment things get out of whack, we have to hold hands and concentrate all our energy on pushing the bad spirit into this lit candle. Do you understand?"

I looked at him, wide-eyed and still completely incredulous. I nodded.

John was silent for some time, and then began to speak to me very quietly. What he said was enough to send shivers down my spine.

"There is a man whirling around this room, he is saying that you are his, and that no one shall have you. He is extremely upset. He wants to possess you. Speak to him, Luci, tell him to leave you in peace!" John said fiercely with closed eyes.

I stared at John. Was he serious? What was I to say?

"Uhh," I started, still not believing what was happening. "I don't want you near me anymore, do you understand? I want peace, so… leave me alone!"

There was a sudden chill in the room, I turned to look at my window: It was closed. Where had the chill come from? I became frightened.

"Okay, he's pretty pissed off now. Say something to really make him understand you want to be left alone!" John shouted.

The candle wavered.

"Uhh, get the hell out of my life! I don't want you anymore!" I yelled. John was silent and then he opened his eyes.

"He's a little boy crying now. He says that he can't live without you."

I shook my head in disbelief. This was like something out of Hollywood.

"Well, I'm sorry, I can't be with you. I love you but can't be with you, so please, return to where you came from and leave me in peace," I said, looking around the room, trying to see something that couldn't be seen with the human eye.

A dead silence answered us. John opened his eyes and said that the boy had a message for me.

"He says to tell you, let the wind blow, let the rivers flow, but never let your heart be forsaken," John said slowly.

My jaw dropped open. I felt the hairs on my nape standing upright because these words were familiar to me. They were almost the exact words Brian had said to me one night, the last night that I had seen him before I had decided never to see him again. He had told me that I should always protect my heart and allow the river of life to flow through me.

"How did you know that?" I said to John. "How did you know that?"

"Know what?"

"Those words, I know those words... Brian told me those words the last night we saw each other! How could you possibly know those exact words? I never told anyone about those words."

John looked at me and smiled.

"I told you, the blond boy told me before he went away."

Chapter 21

After that evening, I didn't have the nightmares again. Grateful, I returned to my peaceful sleep but had trouble trying to understand the mysterious and frightening visions of that October. I spoke to John about it later and he said a few things that made me realize that ghosts are not necessarily dead people; according to him, they could be living people too.

"The living haunt the living, Luci. It's a matter of projecting what we call the astral body out of the real body. I know you're shaking your head, but listen to me: Brian was a real-life vampire. Vampires are not fiction. There are people out there that feed off others, you know, the Nietzsche fly which sucks your blood type-thing? Well, this guy was obviously feeding off your energy field. He made himself stronger through using you. The word 'to use somebody' is quite literal here: He was using you to make himself stronger."

"I don't get it," I responded, shaking my head.

"Yes, well, we live in a scientific world," he said as I shifted uncomfortably in my seat. "People don't believe in stuff like that. They think dreams are random, unimportant figments of our unconscious mind. Basically, trash. Dreams are much more than that! They connect you to the other realms, you know, the invisible realms? I'm sure deep inside you know what I'm talking about. Do you think reality is all about what you see? Weren't those dreams pretty real to you?"

I decided not to bring the subject up again because it was a bit too much for me at the time. I still couldn't understand how a real life person could come and torment me in dreams.

From then on, I had no choice anymore: I had to take a break from men. I couldn't handle another disappointment, and especially not another vampire man, so I focused all my attention on school and getting good grades in my computer courses. At least I was going to succeed in life and make money, and to hell with love.

*   *   *

"I am glad you brought up this concept of vampires, Lucina," Señora Labotta said, taking a long sip of her water. The wine bottle had emptied itself a long time ago. "Indeed, as your friend rightly pointed out, humans can haunt humans too, it is a matter of powerful thought projections. Carlos' mentor talked about this in his books and called this projection 'the double'. One needs to be careful who one connects with, just for the reason that ties can last a lifetime. For instance, they say that one should be careful with whom one sleeps because these ties could last up to seven years. Imagine if you sleep with a lot of men how many ties you have with those men in the invisible realms? Enough to make you quite weak in the physical realm."

Lucina shuddered, remembering the terrible nightmares.

"But please, go on, these stories are so very educating."

*   *   *

Some months later, as I was taking a hard drive apart and trying to figure out where things had gone wrong, I ran into Lincoln. Thinking he was having trouble putting his drive together, I went up to him and offered to help him out with the wiring.

"I don't need help at all, but thanks," he replied, confidently returning to his work.

I shrugged and turned my attention back to my own drive.

Lincoln was very tall and also intimidating upon first en-counter. His dark hazel eyes stared straight into yours and made you somewhat uncomfortable. He had a nice lean muscular body and very short, black hair, was extremely quiet, and kept to himself in the classroom. What fascinated me the most about him was that he had this evasive energy, the kind that flutters around but can never be pinned down. Was he nice, or not? I couldn't tell at all.

I was surprised when he invited me to go to a movie with him one afternoon. At first, I wanted to decline, but when I saw his sudden smile, I couldn't help but say yes.

Luci, what are you doing? the voice said in my head. Con-centrate on school, not boys. Boys mess you up whereas school smartens you up. Focus, Luci.

Pushing the voice out of my mind, I smiled at Lincoln. This time, I knew that I couldn't get side-tracked; enough had hap-pened and I would not lose control. We went together to the movies one cold January afternoon and it didn't take long before we were dating. I made it clear to Lincoln from the beginning that I was damaged goods only looking for a resting spot and that I had no intention of sticking around.

One night, we were kissing passionately when I began to feel the familiar disorientation effect. I stood up right away, told him I needed to talk to him, and led him to his car. We sat in the darkness, the moon shining her frowning face upon us.

"I'm not able to do this," I said slowly, looking away so that Lincoln would not see the fear in my eyes. "You're a great guy, but I just can't do this. I rather stop now before it's too late. I'm sorry."

He turned and gaped at me, searching for the truth in my eyes. I avoided looking at him, and stared out the window. When people lie they have a hard time looking straight into a person's eyes while doing it.

"Luci, I know you are frightened, but that's not an excuse to give up just like that. Why don't you wait and see what happens?" he replied, his body taught.

"I don't have the patience, nor the energy," I replied, clenching my jaw.

Lincoln looked terribly hurt and told me that he had no choice but to accept my decision. I went back inside my apartment feeling empty, sad but safe, and Lincoln drove away into the night. At school he avoided me, but eventually after a few weeks had gone by, we began to talk again, and the familiar fire sparked between us. I promised myself that this time, I wouldn't leave him, that I would just ride the wave, feel no attachment, and enjoy myself.

We dated for a few more weeks, until I began to feel the dreaded feeling of floating downstream once more, that feeling that had brought me so much pain before. The feeling of losing control gripped my heart and I decided to run away from Lincoln again, this time for real. I had promised myself never to lose control again and I was going to keep this promise.

I remember the scene as though it were yesterday. Lincoln was wearing white and was sitting in a lawn chair in his large backyard at his parent's beautiful home. The gentle wind blew lightly in his soft dark hair, and a bright moon hung overhead, looking sullen and depressed.

Hands on hips, I acted the role of the heartless woman to perfection. My words were designed to cut him out of my life for good.

"Lincoln, this is not working out," I spurted out, glaring at him.

He sat silently and calmly, his eyes staring in me. I waited for him to speak. He shifted in the plastic chair, crossed one leg, and finally sighed. His following words pierced my ego, but I tried to act as though he had said nothing to destabilize me.

"You will never find love because you can't surrender. You fight with yourself, you want to love, yet you don't want to surrender. You search for your soul mate but you don't know yourself even. You're making a big mistake here, but I don't care anymore: It's your loss now, not mine. I've given you my love and you've rejected it. Have a good life."

I turned my back to him, pretending that I was shaking from rage and not sadness. I grabbed my sweater from his couch, and ran out of his house before I could collapse into his arms and beg him to be patient with me, beg him to love me even though I couldn't love him back, beg him to see through my pain and scars.

Lincoln refused to see me after that night. I can't blame him for realizing that my world was a world of ruined love and that I was a hopeless case. I crawled back into my hole after him, back in with my machines and my demons.

Part Four
Pandora's Box

Chapter 22

Señora Labotta flicked on the small turquoise table lamp and a bluish soft light filled the quiet living room. Outside the crickets chirped their sad song and a light breeze blew through the open windows into the tranquil, peaceful Mexican house. The clock read 4:06 a.m.

"Luci, your love stories are humanity's love stories," Señora Labotta said softly.

Lucina remained silent.

"I can understand why for you, love is filled with black memories, but please remember that love has no past and no future: It lives in the present moment. That is the second rule in love. For it to survive it needs to be sheltered from the thoughts, the mind; it needs to be nested in the heart and it needs to be left alone. I understand that many humans need to go through rejection and illusions, it is part of their karma if you will, but you cannot allow your past to cloud your future."

"Yes, I see that now too," Lucina replied, sighing. After pouring her heart out, Lucina felt as though the past didn't matter as much anymore. The past seemed like a bad dream that simply needed to be put into words in order to be forgotten.

"Bad love experiences happen to everyone," Señora Labotta continued, staring deep into Lucina's eyes. "You are not the only soul who has suffered in love. There is a saying I like very much, Boethius said this; 'Commit your boat to the winds and you must sail whichever way they blow, not just where you want'. People forget that love is its own wind and that love cannot be controlled. Once you give into love, you are a goner so to speak. Your boat will be rocked, my dear, but eventually you will hit treasure if you persist."

Lucina remained silent and stared out the window. A full moon stared back at her, a moon she thought she recognized from the scene with Lincoln in that garden one night in May.

"Let me teach you something about fear," Señora Labotta said, watching Lucina. "The opposite of love is fear. When you fear something, it is the brain signaling to you that you should not advance, that you should retreat. For example, if you see a snake in the woods, your first instinct will be to retreat. Your brain is telling you this, but why? Because a part of you does not want to evolve, a part of you wants to repeat all the past lives you have lived, and your fear is a mechanism which enables you to repeat endlessly your lives."

"What would happen if you were to go up to the snake, stare it straight in the eye and say to it, 'I am not afraid of you'? You would be breaking the chain of the past and you would be advancing to a new level. Every time you conquer something which you fear, you ascend. The only way to evolve is to ascend. Many people do not face their fears and they run instead, but in running, they are doomed to repeat the past."

Lucina nodded her head. She knew that this was true from experience because she had been repeating the same relationships throughout the years. She had been chasing the wrong men, and for the wrong reasons. Most of the men she had loved had been afraid of love and there was her biggest problem: She had been chasing impossible men, men that didn't believe in true love to begin with.

"How can you know which is the true love, the true mountain?" Lucina asked. Señora Labotta nodded her head, as if she knew Lucina would ask this question.

"You cannot know unless you climb and that is always frightening. But anyone who has faith will be rewarded in the end, even if it is not true love awaiting them. That is the third rule in love."

A firefly buzzed in and spun around the dim light on the table.

"Señorita, it is time to go to bed now, but let us pursue our thoughts tomorrow morning." Señora Labotta said, tiredly. "Thank you for sharing these stories with me tonight; I shall remember them a long time. I do hope you feel as though your heart is somewhat less filled with bloody memories?"

Lucina nodded, not sure if her heart felt anything anymore at all.

Señora Labotta disappeared in her red bedroom, after having wished her guest a good night of rest and recuperation. Lucina made her way quietly to the bathroom, locking the door behind her. She had spent the last few hours telling a perfect stranger her deepest moments of pain and it felt wonderful to finally share it with someone understanding. She looked at the pale face in the mirror and blinked. *What happens after all those men? Is there only bliss now?* she pondered.

She chewed her lower lip and closed her eyes.

I guess there's only one way to find out if Teleo is yet another heart-ache. I have to climb and see what's on top for me, she realized. *What if there's nothing more than pain? Then I must face my fear, not let it get me, not repeat the past. Señora Labotta is right: The reason why the human race is not evolving is because we let fear lead us. Look at the war going on, is that not also ruled by fear, fear of the other? So much fear. So much fear.*

How do I begin to get over my fears? Lucina thought sadly.

She suddenly felt like Alice going down into the rabbit hole.

Chapter 23

Early the next morning, Lucina picked up a pen and wrote the first line of a poem. Then, the rest came rushing into her head, and before long, she had written a whole poem.

Deconstruction

Standing slouched over this beam of wood
My hair dripping metallic chains of blood,
Nothing behind but broken images,
Illusions strewn like worthless cottages.
Amidst the manless, soulless deconstruction
I hold up the white with all the might in me
And scream, "I surrender! O leave and never return!
See you not that all my world is burnt?"

Nothing responds. So I must face the unknown
Again alone; yet now my sword is here
By my trembling side, and my head
Lifts up to the clouds, to my Eternal Life.
One more chance, this mountain calls to me.
The greatest faith is to have faith that love
Shall lift you up, and save you from the world.

Lucina stared at her poem for some time. Señora Labotta's influence is starting to show, she noted to herself. Perhaps writing poetry shall liberate me.

"Luci?" Señora Labotta's voice called from outside the tent. Lucina dropped her pen, closed her diary, quickly popped her head out of the tent, and saw Señora Labotta standing near.

"I want to introduce you to some people, they are visiting with us for some time," Señora Labotta said. Lucina didn't feel like seeing people, but she decided to make an effort. She nodded and replied that she would be there in a minute. Quickly, she grabbed a pair of jeans, a sweater and stepped out into the early morning light.

She trudged up to the house rather unhappy at the thought of having to meet people that early in the morning. Lucina was not a morning person at all. As she came around to the front of the house, she saw three young men unloading various objects from a big blue van. Señora Labotta smiled and signalled for her guest to come closer. Lucina walked over, rather surprised and uneasy. *What is going on?* she thought in a panic. *Who are all these men?*

"Lucina, I would like to present to you my three nephews from Acapulco. They will be staying with us for some days, as they are helping to renovate my house," Señora Labotta explained, as the young men all took their hats off and smiled at Lucina.

Lucina took a deep breath. *Okay, here we go*, she thought. *More men to deal with. I thought Teleo was too much, now there are three new men. When it rains, it pours*, she reminded herself. She took a quick look at the three Mexicans. The one unloading a box was short, bearded and scruffy looking. The tall skinny man next to the car smiled warmly at Lucina, and she smiled back awkwardly. She stopped when she noticed the good-looking man in the back, busy locking the trunk.

"Alberto, Juan and Mathias are all going to be sleeping in their van, so they will not be bothering you, Luci. I hope you will all be friends in no time," said Señora Labotta as she helped her nephews unload their various tools.

"*Encantado, señorita, soy Alberto*" said the short man, as he shook Lucina's hand.

"*Mucho gusto, Juan,*" the tall one said with a smile as they shook hands.

"*Es un placer,*" said the handsome man, walking over to where Lucina stood. She shifted uncomfortably under his taunting smile. "*Me llamo Mathias.*"

She smiled forcefully and excused herself. *A cold shower will do me good,* she mused, heading into the bathroom. *I need a cold shower this morning.* Undressing, she was hit with a terrible thought: What if Teleo didn't return? What if she were stuck there with three men her whole life, waiting for Teleo?

*   *   *

That day, the hammering began. Lucina had always hated loud noises, and on that day she especially wanted to get away. She asked Señora Labotta if she could borrow Luna and Señora Labotta replied that Lucina didn't have to ask. As Lucina saddled up Luna, Mathias appeared out of nowhere, nearly scaring Lucina out of her wits.

"*Dónde vas?*" he asked her, wiping his hands on his dirty overalls.

"For a ride," she answered, without looking at him directly. Mathias smiled and shrugged.

"Just when you want some beautiful company, they ride off with another. Oh well, *es la vida!*" he said, putting his hands up to the sky.

Lucina turned bright red, smiled awkwardly and quickly trotted away on Luna's hard back.

The jungle was cool and moist that morning as she slowly made her way into the thick trees. A faint soothing rustling sound greeted Lucina and Luna as they made their way deeper into the jungle. The sound of exotic birds surrounded them, and she couldn't help but feel as though the only true place in the world then was the jungle. Lucina looked up at the large green leaves shading Luna and her from the sun, and thought how wonderful it was not to be surrounded by people, noise and confusion.

Sssssssssssssssssssss.

Stiffening, Lucina stopped breathing and clenched the reins in her trembling hands, feeling the sweat begin to form on her forehead. She looked around her nervously, pulling on the reins so that Luna would stop.

Evidently, snakes are inescapable, Lucina thought miserably. She closed her eyes tightly and prayed out loud that the snake would go away. But then she heard the familiar hissing sound again. Slowly opening her eyes, she spotted the infamous yellow and red strips, entwined in a heap some ten feet away from where they had stopped.

The snake lay right in the middle of the path.

Lucina was about to turn her horse around, when all of a sudden, Señora Labotta's booming voice came into her head; "Every time you conquer something which you fear, you ascend. The only way to evolve is to ascend. Many people do not face their fears and they run instead." Hadn't Señora Labotta told her about facing snakes just yesterday? *What a crazy coincidence,* Lucina realized. She took a deep breath and slid off of Luna. The snake hissed again, as if warning Lucina to keep away. She crept slowly up to where it lay and knees shaking, she spoke to it, as though in a dream.

"Okay, snake. Here we are, face to face, and I am not running away. If indeed you are my sexual awakening, I guess I can't run away from it anymore. I have to deal with it. Well, I forgive you for the bite the other night and hope you don't have to do that again."

The snake hissed at Lucina, then, silently, it slithered off the trail and vanished into the bushes. Lucina watched it disappear, a feeling of warmth going through her.

"Well, that wasn't so hard, now Luna, was it?" Lucina said, relieved as she climbed back unto her horse. "Now I know why old women talk to their cats. Talking liberates them."

Luna whinnied in response.

Chapter 24

The meeting with the snake left a magical imprint on Lucina. She wanted desperately to share the experience with Señora Labotta, yet every time she went towards her, Señora Labotta was busy with the renovations, so Lucina decided not to mention the incident to her.

She found the courage to begin working in the bookstore one Tuesday afternoon. She was not used to speaking Spanish fluently, but after a few days, the language seemed to make more sense to her. Lucina slowly began to enjoy the dusty smell of manuscripts and the familiar scent of Indian incense in the store. She befriended quickly the other two employees, both elderly women who spoke very little English, and they mainly got along in the beginning with hand signals and dictionaries.

At night, Lucina would take the bus home and eat supper with Señora Labotta and her three nephews. They would drink beer, laugh and tell stories. The men especially liked to hear Lucina talk about Canada and what type of life Canadians led. Lucina promised them that if they ever wanted to visit, her mother would welcome them as she was learning to be a true Christian.

Lucina soon became conscious of Mathias' interest, but she feigned ignorance, and turned her attention to searching for a cheap apartment near Señora Labotta's house. She also busied herself with weeding, cooking and cleaning up after the renovations each day.

One night, as Lucina was walking to her tent from Señora

Labotta's newly painted forest green home, Mathias appeared on the dirt path ten feet in front of her. Lucina jumped when she saw his silhouette in the darkness.

"*Hola, señorita. Dónde vas?*" he asked, gently.

Crickets chirped in the darkness around them.

"Going to bed," Lucina responded calmly, trying to discern his features in the shadows.

Mathias walked quietly closer to her. At that moment, a soft gust of wind gently played in his hair.

"You know, I was wondering the other night about something. Is there a story between you and Teleo?" he said, as he emerged from the shadows.

Lucina bit her lip, uncertain as to what to reply. *Why is he asking this?* she thought. *He surely wants to know if he can make a move. Oh no, this is trouble.*

"Well, I will tell you that when I see Teleo again," Lucina answered, trying to sound calm. She was certainly not going to go into details with this stud.

The moonlight hit Mathias's elegant brown face and his blue shining eyes stared directly into Lucina's. He was wearing faded blue jeans, torn at the knees, and a sleeveless white top, slightly opened at the top, revealing his hairless chest beneath.

As he came closer to her, Lucina felt her pulse begin to race.

"Now, señorita, can you be certain that you like Teleo very much? And not me let's say?" he said in a hoarse voice, as he came even closer to where she was standing. Unexpectedly, he was right in front of her, too close for comfort. Lucina felt dizzy, and looked around her to find a focal point on which she could rest her eyes to regain her sense of orientation. When only darkness and shadows greeted her, she turned her eyes back to Mathias and looked into his eyes without flinching.

His right hand came up to touch her cheek. She wanted to pull back, run away, but something was keeping her rooted in place. Her mind began to race. Fragments of thoughts entered her and seemed to add to the chaos. When his face drew nearer to hers, Lucina shivered in the warm evening and felt her body begin to stir. Gently, his large hand caressed her cheek, and she felt his other hand pressing on her back. He brought his body closer to hers. *What are you doing, Lucina?* screamed the voice inside her. *Turn the switch back on!*

"Hermosa Lucina, tan hermosa. Eres una flora de Canada..." his voice whispered to Lucina from the darkness.

His body came up confidently against Lucina's and she felt a familiar heat surging through her veins. His lips were almost brushing hers, when out of the darkness appeared Teleo's beautiful green eyes. Her senses came back to her.

"Mathias!" she shouted loudly, beside herself.

Mathias, surprised, jumped back.

"Please, don't do this. I find you very attractive, but I am waiting for Teleo. Please, let me go."

Mathias fumbled backwards as though Lucina had slapped him. She saw the hurt look on his face. Sighing, she closed her eyes and re-opened them. He was still standing there: It had not been a vision.

"No comprendo, pensaba que..." he said slowly.

Lucina sighed again and explained to Mathias that she couldn't do this. She told him that she wasn't chasing air anymore. Mathias looked at her, dumb-founded, but she didn't give him a further explanation, she merely walked past him quickly, making sure to avoid touching him again. Lucina nearly ran to her tent, stumbled inside, closed the zipper, and fell back unto her sleeping bag. She closed her eyes and tried to ignore the blood rushing through her veins, her heart beating quickly, her sweaty palms.

Attraction is so powerful, she thought, catching her breath. *I think I need to question Señora Labotta on the subject of attraction tomorrow morning, just to orient myself better.*

*   *   *

That night, Lucina dreamt that she was surrounded by classical music. Lovely, soft violin played in her ears. She was in a music hall, surrounded by many people dressed in Victorian style, seated in a thick red cushioned seat. She focused on the scene in front of her, trying to see who was playing the music. When she turned to ask someone next to her who the musicians were, Mathias greeted her. He was wearing a green tailored suit, with a black top hat and had a white rose stuck in the pocket of his coat.

"Who are the musicians?" he asked Lucina, playing with her hair, a discreet smile playing across his red lips.

"I don't know."

"Yes, you know. They are the ones playing the music. See, over there," he responded, pointing to a few beautiful naked men playing violin. Lucina glanced over and noticed that the men were extremely well-built, tanned, tall and Greek-looking. Each one looked like a Michelangelo sculpture.

"Such is the question we face: Are we made to be monogamous or are we made to be polygamous?" Mathias asked, putting his arm around her. Lucina shivered and wanted to take his arm away, but she didn't move.

"I don't know," she replied again, fascinated by the army of beauty.

In a blink of an eye, Lucina was standing amidst the naked violinists, they were playing for her, and she was dancing slowly. She felt Mathias pull her to him and closed her eyes, welcoming his hot lips.

"Why are we polygamous in our dreams and not in reality?" he murmured in her ears.

He began to undress her to the beat of the inviting music. The lights dimmed and they were in a field of daisies, making love under the moonlit sky.

"Stop, Mathias, stop," Lucina murmured in his ear. He laughed and whispered that there was no difference between loving him or loving Teleo.

Lucina awoke with a jump.

Looking around her tent, she half-expected to see Mathias sitting near her, observing her. When she realized that she was alone, Lucina fell back unto her pillow, sighing loudly.

"Holy crap," she said. "I really need to talk to Señora Labotta."

*　　*　　*

Señora Labotta was eating pancakes the next morning when Lucina arrived in the kitchen. She looked up, smiled, and invited Lucina to join her.

"How are you, señorita? You look like you did not sleep well."

Lucina shifted in her seat, unsure of how to begin.

"I have been wondering, Señora, about the nature of human attraction. Should we be only with one man at a time, or is it possible to be with several men and still all love them equally?"

Señora Labotta slowly put down her fork, wiped her mouth with her napkin and cleared her throat.

"Lucina," she began in a soft tone, "Attraction is one thing, love is another. You can be attracted to many men and women, but to love them is different. In love we connect soul, mind and body. In attraction, usually it's just the body. In general, life brings one powerful mirror at a time because it makes no sense to have our soul mates all at the same time; we would be more confused than ever. No, one soul mate at a time, that is my belief. So pick the most powerful one, the one you feel will teach you more than the others and stick with him. If it ends one day, be open to the next one. There is always a next one, until we become enlightened."

She stopped a second to let Lucina ponder her words.

"But of course, as you pointed out, it is tempting to look at all the men. It is tempting to imagine them naked and on top of us. But that is just the physical part in us, the weakest link. Just imagine you were dating ten men all at once, how could you possibly give yourself fully to each man and not get lost in the process? Those that say polygamy is the way of the world are deluded by their desire to possess every beautiful thing on this earth. They are driven by their egos, or they are simply afraid of commitment."

"I understand what you're saying," Lucina responded, "But what if you loved just two men? Would *that* be so bad?"

Señora Labotta laughed.

"If you love two men, you will be divided, inevitably. Half of you with one, and the other half of you with the other. Do you enjoy being divided?"

Lucina shook her head.

"Well, if you do not like to be divided, then choose the best man and give your full attention to him. I would not be surprised if that man turns out to be the best mirror for you. How to choose the best man? Follow that voice within you, listen to it attentively, that voice comes from your heart."

She got up with a smile, cleared the table, and invited Lucina for a walk in the woods.

The two women went down the steps of the newly renovated house and strolled towards the shade of the jungle. It was a humid day, but the wind cooled them off, making their walk more enjoyable. Lucina noticed how Señora Labotta walked with a lightness of foot. It was strange that such a heavy woman made no sound as she walked.

"You know, once I met a young man while Teleo's father was away on business," Señora Labotta began. "He was very charming, and very direct, if you know what I mean. One night, he offered to drive me home after a village party and I accepted. When he arrived at my home, he took my hand and kissed it. I felt very much alive then, as though all my cells had magically awakened. I wanted to continue our contact, but then Teleo's father's face flashed before my eyes and I knew that if I proceeded, I would be killing our beautiful spiritual journey together."

They entered the jungle, unto the narrow dirt path. Birds squawked loudly around them, as if trying to catch their attention.

"I knew that if I gave into my impulses, I would destroy something precious. I chose Teleo's father, and I never regretted it; he turned out to be my greatest teacher."

Lucina remained silent, turning over the recent evening scene with Mathias in her mind.

How to start listening to my heart? she wondered. *I hear so many voices all the time, how to know which one is from the heart and not from the Tormentor?* She decided to ask the Mexican.

"How can I tell which voice is from the heart and which voice is from my head?"

Señora Labotta laughed. She patted Lucina on the shoulder, laughing again.

"It takes time, my dear, and a lot of patience. Usually the heart stirs before the mind even registers anything. Try to be silent more, you will have fewer voices confusing you, and one day, you'll just have the heart speaking. It is quite simple; usually it says yes or it says no. Yes to this man, no to the other."

Lucina doubted it was so simple.

*   *   *

Lucina saw Mathias that evening, drinking a beer in the back with Albert and Juan. When she approached, Mathias said something in Spanish and jogged up to where Lucina was standing.

"*Venga,* let's walk," he said, putting his beer on a crooked picnic table. Lucina followed him, knowing full well that she could not escape their conversation. They went to the road and walked side by side in silence for a few moments. Mathias walked with his hands in his khaki short pockets, while Lucina observed the setting sun.

"I'm sorry about last night," he began slowly. "I should have never done that, and I apologize. I understand that you have feelings for Teleo now. It's just that men are more *animales* than women, you know?"

Lucina nodded, surprised at his honesty. *At long last, one man who can admit his sexual impulses, a good thing,* she reflected happily. *If they could all just admit what they are after, it would make our lives much easier.* Mathias grinned back.

"You know, men are easy to analyze. If we talk to you, it's because we want you in our bed. If we say hello to you, it's because we want you in our bed too. Most of the time, anyhow!"

Lucina shook her head, grinning.

"Mathias, I appreciate your honesty. I find you very attractive, and I wouldn't have minded being with you. But the thing is, I think I have found a true mirror, and I don't intend on messing it up. Not this time, anyhow."

Mathias smiled, and began walking again.

"I wish that I had found you before, maybe you would be saying those words about me instead of about Teleo. *Que piensas?*" he said softly.

"I think that timing is everything," Lucina replied, looking up at the purple and pink clouds. She had learned that much in the past.

"So, you plan on marrying him someday?"

Lucina stopped walking and turned to give him a long look.

"Marriage is a whole other subject," she said mysteriously.

*   *   *

Albert, Juan and Mathias left the following day. Before leaving, Mathias took Lucina aside and whispered in her ear that if ever she changed her mind, she knew where to find him. She patted him on the shoulder and replied that without a doubt, she would not forget his honest effort to win her. *The grass is always greener on the other side*, she repeated to herself as she watched his handsome figure vanish into the early morning rays.

Lucina went to work at the bookstore that day and fell upon a torn copy of *Wuthering Heights*. Haphazardly, she flipped open the book out of curiosity.

"Very gloomy book," erupted Elena's thick, coarse Spanish voice from behind her. "A book about love should never be gloomy, because there has been enough gloomy love on this planet. Hmph, what people write should not frustrate the readers but should elevate them."

Lucina jumped and put the book down. Elena always had the ability to sneak up on anyone and make them jump.

"Why do love books always have to be so tortured?" Elena called out again. She had a few copies of books in her hand, and dumped them in front of Lucina on the counter like potatoes. "Look at this, Shakespeare's *Winter's Tale*. Great book about jealousy and the results of jealousy. And this one, by George Orwell called *1984*, ends with the system winning over love. The list is endless. Love is a disaster in literature. Look at Ovid's stories; they all end in the woman being ravished because men can't control their penises. Humans have written long enough about the downfall of love."

Lucina laughed and shook her head.

"The human race needs elevation, I agree Elena," Lucina replied, helping Elena place new books on the shelf.

Chapter 25

When Teleo called a few days later, at the same time, a storm hit the valley. The wind tore through the cracks in the small house, and strange, eerie, moaning sounds permeated the dwelling. Rain beat against the small windows, giving Lucina the impression that something dark and menacing was lurking outside, trying to get in.

Teleo spoke first to his mother and then Lucina had a chance to speak with him. She felt her stomach contract as she picked up the receiver. For a few minutes, Teleo chatted about his job in the village, explaining that the epidemic was spreading fast and that many people had died of the fever in the last few days. He explained that he was feeling frustrated but also confident in the end that he would help the village.

When Teleo had finished talking, Lucina gave him a summary of her last few days in Oaxaca. Of course, she avoided telling him about Mathias, knowing that it was no use speaking about things that would never materialize; Mathias had been a shadow and had left as magically as he had appeared. Teleo asked her how she was enjoying the new job at the store and she responded that she was learning a lot about literature, especially from the grumbling Elena. Teleo laughed and warned her to stay away from Elena because she had a habit of convincing others easily.

Then Teleo said something Lucina wished he hadn't. He mentioned that there was a woman assisting him in the field, a

Mexican woman named Josefina. Lucina's ears pricked up, and
she decided to probe him further.

"Is she nice?" Lucina asked, twisting the phone cord around
her hand. An image of a beautiful, dark-headed goddess appeared in her mind. She pictured the nurse in a tight little skirt
and high-heels, bending over a patient and winking at Teleo. *My
God*, she thought nervously. *What if he really is not interested in me
and has his eyes on someone else already? What then?*

"Very nice, Lucina," he answered. "Josefina is very competent
and very methodical. Thank God we have her here." She wanted
to ask him more about his "assistant" but decided it would be
too evident she was uncomfortable. *Pull yourself together,* she told
herself. *Pull yourself together.*

They talked a few more minutes and then Lucina hung up.
She sat down on the couch, sighed and stared up at the ceiling.
She felt like kicking the living room table in front of her.

*Who the heck is Josefina? Is she trying to seduce Teleo at that mo-
ment, her legs crossed seductively, smoking a long cigarette, staring
into his green eyes? Is she playing with her hair, hoping Teleo will soon
have his fingers entangled in it? Is she…*

"Would you like some wine, señorita? You look like you need
a glass," interrupted a deep voice. Lucina jumped at the sound
of Señora Labotta's penetrating voice. She smiled forcefully, accepted the glass with relief and took a long sip.

"I could not help but over-hear that Teleo has a friend in
Guatemala?"

Lucina lifted her eye brows a little, trying to smile. Her
stomach contracted. She felt like she was back in France, living
the same nightmare. There she was, in another country, waiting
for love to arrive. Had she done the same mistake again, had she
been too impulsive? Was she reverting back to her original teen-
age behavior?

Oh calm down, the voice whispered. *Your fears are getting the better of you again. Remember: Where there is no fear, there is love.*

Señora Labotta sat down next to her guest, taking a sip of her wine. She patted Lucina's arm reassuringly, like she had done the first day Lucina had returned to find that her son was gone.

"Let me describe you something and you tell me what is wrong with it," the Mexican woman said, clearing her throat loudly. Lucina took a long sip of the French wine and nodded. "There is a woman playing in a field. She is prancing around, light as a feather, happy and content because there is a man next to her. They play like children for many days and many months. The sun is always shining, the weather always warm, and the field always flowery. Tell me, what is wrong with this picture?"

"I don't know," Lucina answered, curious as to what Señora Labotta would say next.

"I will tell you what is wrong. This is a fairy tale vision of love, and it does not exist. Girls grow up with this picture in their minds very early on. They think that when they will find their soul mate, all will be like a fairy tale; birds will always chirp, the sun will always shine, the weather will always be warm. Unfortunately, all this is horse crap. It does not exist. What does exist is what I call Pandora's Box. What happens when you finally meet your soul mate, or one of them, is that a chest opens, the one that has been locked up for so much time. Guess what is released?"

Lucina shook her head, uncertain of what to answer.

"What is first released from Pandora's Box? I will tell you the actual myth then. Pandora, in Greek mythology, was a woman bestowed with many gifts by various Gods. She was sent to man as a poisoned gift and she carried with her a jar. In her jar, there were many evils stored inside. Zeus warned her never to open her jar, but Pandora became curious and eventually opened the jar, releasing all types of evils into the world. True love, if we are lucky enough to find it, is truly like this at the beginning; our chests are opened and out come all the little demons. We are horrified and want to run away as soon as we see this, because no one has told us about Pandora's Box."

Lucina leaned forward on the couch, staring at Señora Labotta intensely. Her interest had been roused and she wanted to know what happened after.

"The second stage is hope. When Pandora returned to her jar once more, hope escaped from it. Thus it is said that in times of darkness there is always hope. At first then, love opens that locked chest inside of us and releases all our little demons, but the most important thing that it releases is hope. You might live through jealousy, envy, insecurity, and distrust, but always remember: There is hope somewhere in your chest."

Lucina sat silently looking at the now empty wine glass in her hand. Josefina came back in her mind and she shifted uncomfortably at the vision.

"So, how do we know what is stored in that chest inside of us, I mean, before we fall in love? Is there some sort of Pandora Box Indicator I don't know about?" Lucina said, getting more and more depressed by the minute. Señora Labotta laughed a hearty laugh.

"Ah, you Canadians! You always think that science will save your souls. There is no indicator; there is only time and courage. You need to be courageous, and stand in the storm, face the music so to speak. Who knows how many demons are in your jar? Maybe you have one, or maybe a hundred. You will know when you really fall in love because that is when the surprises come."

"Is there a remedy for killing the demons even before the chest is opened?" Lucina asked.

"None whatsoever, only courage, as I mentioned beforehand. What happens often is most humans have no clue what they are getting themselves into when they meet their soul mates. They see Hollywood movies, the flowers floating around everywhere, the 'Happy Ever After' moments, couples walking hand in hand in the street and looking like they have no problems, no conflicts, no wounds. But remember that nothing is what it seems and that there are many layers of reality all around us, however, there are simple rules to guide us, which we all know more or less. Remember the rules I taught you?"

Lucina nodded, filling her glass again.

"The first is patience. The second is that love lives only in the present moment. The third is that anyone who has faith in love shall be rewarded, even if it is the wrong love. The fourth and last rule, which is more a stage than a rule, is when you meet your soul mate, you meet all aspects of yourself, even the demons buried deep within. Remember that the last stage is the one which no one can help you with."

"This sounds like hell!" Lucina blurted out, unable to contain herself any longer. Outside the wind howled as though to confirm her words. Señora Labotta laughed loudly, lifting her glass up into the air for a toast. Lucina joined her, raising her glass as well.

"Welcome to the reality of love, my dear: There are no fairy tales. In order to find your soul mate, you must be a warrior of love, and not all humans are warriors from birth. But, I have faith in you yet."

Lucina grinned all of a sudden, realizing how terrifically frightening love was after all. She felt like she was falling off a precipice and unsure of whether she was going to land on rock or on a soft bed of roses.

It's all about having courage, isn't it? she told herself. *Without courage, love can never blossom. I don't want to run away again, I want to face the storm, be a warrior of love.*

"A toast to Lucina's Pandora's Box," Señora Labotta said with a grin. "May it empty itself out quickly and lead her to her inner light eventually."

They toasted merrily and Lucina emptied her glass.

"One last thing, Señora. Do you think I have many demons inside of me?" Lucina asked Señora Labotta sheepishly.

"Ah, time will tell, my dear, time will tell. Now, the best thing to do is sit back and enjoy the fireworks. Well, on that note, I wish you a lovely evening, I am off to bed."

Señora Labotta got up, waved good-night to her guest, and disappeared into her bedroom.

Lucina stopped smiling and was hit by a terrible feeling of loneliness. The rain beat down on the house violently, as if wanting to tear it apart. She stared outside and gulped. *Sleeping through a storm, alone in a tent?* she mused. *Well, I have to begin to be a warrior sometime, right? And it is the perfect night to start my training.*

She left her wine glass on the table and grabbed her woolen green sweater. *Better hurry to the tent, before the wind can sweep me away,* she reasoned.

*   *   *

The storm lasted all night. At times, Lucina had the impression the wind would carry her tent away and that she would never return whole. She wrapped her arms around herself, cradling herself, praying that the storm would pass quickly so that she could sleep. When the wind finally stopped lashing at the tent, the sun was beginning to rise in the east.

Lucina hadn't slept a wink.

Grumpily, she unzipped the tent, stood outside on the wet grass and groaned.

"Good God, how does one survive love?" she said to the nature around her. Pieces of branches were scattered everywhere on the land, as well as leaves and debris. Around her tent she noticed that some of the flowers had been uprooted and certain small palm trees had even been ripped out of the ground.

All of a sudden, the first rays of sunshine appeared over

the horizon, and for a split moment, Lucina was blinded by the bright light coming from the east.

She closed her eyes and took a deep breath.

"Ready or not, love, here I come."

About the Author

Nora Caron was born in Montreal, Quebec. As a child, she traveled to many countries with her family, developing a love early on for culture, people, and art. In Junior College, Nora took up photography and film, and worked as a photo-journalist for two Quebec magazines. She was also the editor of her college newspaper, *The Edge*. In 2001, she was awarded with Best Photographer Award at Champlain College. At twenty, Nora entered university in Psychology but soon turned to English Literature, where she fell in love with Shakespeare's works. She graduated from McGill University in 2006 with a B.A in English Literature and a minor in Spanish and German. In 2010 Nora graduated from Concordia University with a Masters degree in English Literature. Her specialty is Renaissance literature. She speaks fluent French, English, Spanish and German.

Nora has many passions in life. She is one of the three founders of Oceandoll Productions, a Los Angeles-based film production company. Nora has acted in several short films to date and has written a feature Western called "Wyoming Sky" with Ingo Neuhaus, which is currently in development.

New Dimensions of Being, the sequel to *Journey to the Heart*, is due out in November 2013. Nora's novels mix spirituality, philosophy, and history. They are pieces of her life mixed with insights from spiritual teachers she had the opportunity to work with. Nora's stories carry timeless messages that will uplift and empower those who read them.

visit www.noracaron.com for more information

HOMEBOUND
PUBLICATIONS

At Homebound Publications we recognize the importance of going home to gather from the stores of old wisdom
to help nourish our lives in this modern era. We choose to
lend voice to those individuals who endeavor to translate the
old truths into new context and keep alive through the written word ways of life that are now endangered. Our titles introduce insights concerning mankind's present internal, social
and ecological dilemmas.

It is our intention at Homebound Publications to revive
contemplative storytelling. We publish full-length introspec-
tive works of: non-fiction, essay collections, epic verse, short
story collections, journals, travel writing, and novels. In our
fiction titles our intention is to introduce new perspectives
that will directly aid mankind in the trials we face at present.

It is our belief that the stories humanity lives by give both
context and perspective to our lives. Some older stories, while
well-known to the generations, no longer resonate with the
heart of the modern man nor do they address the present situ-
ation we face individually and as a global village. Homebound
chooses titles that balance a reverence for the old sensibilities;
while at the same time presenting new perspectives by which
to live.

CPSIA information can be obtained at www.ICGtesting.com
Printed in the USA
LVOW05s1557120713

342665LV00002B/236/P